To my husband, Roger

whose love and support
are behind every word

THE WITCH'S PORTRAITS

THE WITCH'S PORTRAITS

Lisa Geurdes Mullarkey

DIAL BOOKS FOR YOUNG READERS

NEW YORK

Published by Dial Books for Young Readers
A member of Penguin Putnam Inc.
345 Hudson Street
New York, New York 10014

Library of Congress Cataloging in Publication Data
Mullarkey, Lisa Geurdes.
The witch's portraits/Lisa Geurdes Mullarkey.—1st ed.
p.   cm.
Summary: When twelve-year-old Laura and her friend Cara
discover that their neighbor is a witch who entraps her enemies
in portraits, the girls attempt to free the victims.
ISBN 0-8037-2337-7
[1. Witchcraft—Fiction. 2. Horror stories.] I. Title.
PZ7.M9115Wi 1998 [Fic]—dc21 97-44219 CIP AC

THE WITCH'S PORTRAITS

A True Story

Usually I make my stories up. I can make a story up about anything—a perfectly ordinary fly humming on the wall or a half-eaten baloney sandwich lying on a plate. Anything. And it'll be a good story.

But this story isn't one that I made up.

This is a true story.

It's about a witch, a very unusual witch, a witch who lived in the house right next to mine, and what she did to my best friend, Cara Hadaway, one unforgettable Halloween.

3

Cara and Me

My name is Laura Adson, and when this story happened, I was twelve. Cara, who lived around the block from me, was twelve too.

If you asked me, I'd say that Cara and I were destined to be best friends. I mean, there were all these things that pushed us together, like our ages and the nearness of our houses. Also, besides my older sister, Lucy, there were no other girls in our neighborhood. It was the craziest thing, but every time a baby was born on our street, it was always a boy. Our neighborhood was simply teeming with boys.

Once I asked Cara if she thought this might have something to do with our drinking water. I thought this was a pretty logical question, but Cara only looked at me, rolled her eyes, and said, "Laura, you're such a moron."

My sister, Lucy, was always telling her friends how she lived on this really cool block, while I was always saying exactly the opposite. Before Cara moved into our neighborhood, I hated going outside, because those boys never left me alone. They were always chasing me with snowballs, garden hoses, or wads of chewed gum. The hoses and snowballs were bearable, but that gum was the worst. I used to wear my hair in braids just so it wouldn't stick. One time, though, I forgot, and this creep, Greg Mox, who later became our paperboy, nailed me with grape Bazooka. It took my mother hours to get that stinky purple glob out with olive oil, so she wouldn't have to cut my hair. I still can't chew grape gum. The smell of it alone makes me ill, it really does.

In case you haven't already guessed, I wasn't a very tough kid. Actually, I was a bit of a wimp. I didn't like fights, and I wasn't too crazy about bullies either. But Cara loved a juicy fight, and she herself was something of a bully. Even though it went against my timid nature, I think that's part of the reason I liked her so much. I mean, it's easy to like a bully when she's on your side. And it's even easier if you're scrawny, like me.

If there's one thing I learned from Cara, it's that being tough certainly has some significant advantages. Nobody teased her about her bike, which was one of those old one-speeds you hardly ever see anymore—with wide fenders trimmed with crumbly brown rust—that squeaked when she rode it. None of the boys on our block tossed water balloons at her or threatened to stick gum in her hair. They didn't dare. They knew what she had done to Greg Mox when he called her Four Eyes. Just for the record, she busted Mox's bike and gave him a black eye. After that there wasn't a boy in our neighborhood who'd mess with her—or me, for that matter.

Cara claimed that I looked like a patsy, whatever that is. I was rather small and thin, and I had blue eyes and long, pale-yellow hair like Lucy and my mother. Cara was several inches taller than me, and she was big. Not fat, but thick and sturdy like the trunk of a tree. Her hair was the color of dark chocolate, and it flopped over her forehead and curled in at her neck. She wore glasses, which magnified her hazel eyes.

Cara's complexion was much darker than mine. Her skin was a pale olive color, a few shades lighter than her eyes. The summer before she disappeared, Cara had a dark, nutty tan and I was gold. Every afternoon, when I was done with tennis clinic and she was back from the library, we lay around my pool reading or telling each other stories.

Storytelling was our favorite pastime. It was what held us together; it was what made us best friends.

The last thing I ought to tell you about Cara is that she was unbelievably smart—so smart that she skipped the third grade, and she never had to study to do well on tests. Cara only had to read something once to learn it. And she read everything. I'm sure there wasn't a book in the library that she hadn't at least skimmed with her enormous eyes.

Dove's Cove

Our hometown, Dove's Cove, is nestled in Connecticut. Though Dove's Cove is pretty large, it has a country feel. There are lots of trees and hills, and ponds, creeks, skunks, and foxes.

Most of the people who live in Dove's Cove are rolling in money, and their homes are so big that a hundred people could live in one house without getting on each other's nerves. Practically all the houses are old, and they're set back from the road so that you can't get a good look at them.

I lived with my mother, my father, and Lucy in a white Colonial with black shutters and a brick stoop, path, and wall. Though we weren't millionaires or anything, our house was large. Even so, my sister and I still managed to annoy each other. Lucy, who is four years older than me, was a phone hog and a pest. Whenever I was on the phone, she picked it up about a million times to ask me when I was getting off, which really bothered me. Also, she was always barging into my room to ask me if I liked her crazy outfits. I didn't mind her asking, I just wished that once in a while she'd knock!

Although Cara lived on a pretty fancy street, her house was tiny. Since it was very small and sat in the backyard of a mansion, everyone called it "the cottage." With its faded gray stones, its slanted slate roof, and its many checkered windows, the two-story structure looked like it belonged in England. Still, as charming as it was, I was glad that *I* didn't live in it. I was sure

I'd never get a wink of sleep. Behind the cottage, over a low stone wall, there was a creepy old graveyard. Even though the graveyard belonged to a church, and even though you could see the church sitting like a silver swan in the distance, I always got the feeling that it was loaded with restless ghouls. Cara claimed that the graveyard didn't bother her, but I often wondered if spirits slipped into her room at night and whispered into her ear, filling her head with lots of spooky ideas.

Cara didn't have a mother or any sisters or brothers, and I guess, in a way, that was a good thing, because there weren't a lot of rooms in that cottage. Sometimes, just for fun, I'd try to imagine what Cara would do if she had someone like Lucy living there with her. I was sure she'd go nuts. But as it was, the only people who lived in the cottage were Cara, her father, and an old springer spaniel named Nimbo. Most of the time Cara was alone with Nimbo, because her father was either teaching or at what my father calls "tree-hugger marches."

Mr. Hadaway wasn't like any father I knew. He wasn't at all like *my* father, who was regular, normal—almost like an advertisement for a father. Mr. Hadaway was quirky. With his long limbs he reminded me of a marionette—all dangly bones. While Cara was wild about junk food—constantly stuffing her face with burgers and fries—Mr. Hadaway was a health-food nut. He ate foods with strange, unappetizing names like tofu and soy. And whenever his nose wasn't buried in a book, either he was marching to save some sort of endangered species or forest, or else he was riding his bike.

My parents were always complaining that they spent half their lives in the car, but even though Mr. Hadaway had a car, he rode his bike almost everywhere. He even rode it to work. Once, when my bus was late, I saw him pedaling that old, rickety contraption of his down the street, toward the college where he taught. He was quite a sight, his long hair streaming behind him like the tail of a kite, his ratty tweed jacket all yanked up at the sleeves, and his gray trousers stuffed into a pair of checkered socks. He had strapped his beat-up briefcase to the back of the bike with a bungee cord. I watched Mr. Hadaway strain against the wind, and I wondered why on earth he didn't just drive a car like everyone else.

Once I got up my nerve and asked Cara why her father was so crazy about that ridiculous old bike.

"He rides it," she said, "because he's obsessed with the environment and doesn't want to use up natural resources, like gas and oil. Which is a lot of garbage, Laura, because, if you ask me, those resources are here for us to use." You'd think that some of her father's environmental concerns would've rubbed off on her, but

Cara didn't give a hoot about the environment. She tossed her soda cans into the trash and let her candy wrappers flip-flop down the street.

"Besides," she said, her voice somewhat softer, "that bike was a gift."

"Really?" I asked, genuinely interested. "Who from?"

"My mom. Now cut the questions!"

Mrs. Hadaway died when Cara was five. I always felt pretty awful about that—about Mrs. Hadaway not being around and all. But whenever I brought up the subject, Cara gave me a dirty look and told me to shut my mouth. She didn't like to talk about her mother. I didn't even know what Mrs. Hadaway was like. Once, though, I saw a picture of her on Mr. Hadaway's bedroom dresser. I knew right away that it was Cara's mom. She looked kind of nice. You could see a gentleness in her eyes and in the corners of her small half smile. Her eyes were hazel like Cara's, but whereas Cara's eyes were bright, lively, and sharp, Mrs. Hadaway's were faraway and dreamy. When Cara found me staring at the picture, she snatched it from my hands, turned it facedown, and pulled me out of the room.

Cara's Witch Kick

It was the Monday of the last week of summer vacation. The countdown had begun—seven more days till school. Outside it was humid and hot and eerily still. Nothing moved through the stifling air, not a bug, nor a bird, nor a golf ball. My father's golf clubs lay smoldering on the back lawn. Cara and I were trying to learn how to play golf, though we weren't having a whole lot of success.

Learning golf had been Cara's idea.

"If you can play a good game of golf, Laura," she declared, "you can go anywhere in the world." All summer Cara had been talking about how she wanted to go places, how she wanted to be powerful, famous. For me the future was less distinct. I could barely envision my first day back at school.

"When I grow up, I want to be a big corporate exec with lots of minions," Cara had told me once.

"What's a minion?" I'd asked. It sounded like a little fish, like a minnow.

"A minion, Laura," she replied haughtily, "is an underling—someone you can boss around." She smiled a strong, domineering smile.

Minion. I thought about that word. I rolled it around in my mind. In a way, I hadn't been that far off: Perhaps a minnow was a minion—a tiny fish in a great big sea.

Cara claimed that if you wanted to be a good golfer, you had to start early. The way it looked to me, she was already twelve years too late. She was awful. She kept hitting the ball into the pool. She just never stopped long enough to concentrate.

"She stays in that house all day long," Cara said, handing me a putter. "What does an old lady like her do in there?"

"Who?" I asked, though I knew she was talking about my next-door neighbor, old Mrs. Blackert.

Cara nudged me so that the putter slid in my hands. It collided with the ball, sending it directly into my mother's flowerbed. "You know who!" she hollered.

I glared at her. "Now look what you made me do!" I moaned. My mother goes bonkers when anyone messes with her flowers.

"You did that yourself, Laura." Cara pushed her glasses up her nose. She was always doing that, because they were always sliding down. She swore that next year, when she turned thirteen and was a full-fledged teenager, she'd get contacts.

She snatched the putter from me, bent down, and removed one of the white balls from its package. She dropped the ball onto the tired summer grass and hit it, for the hundredth time, into the pool. It entered the perfectly smooth water with a loud plop, then sank to the bottom.

"Come on, Laura, answer me. What do you think

Mrs. Blackert does all day?" Cara was angry now, angry that her putt had been worse than mine.

Very carefully I wedged my foot between a petunia and a daylily and picked up my wayward ball. "I guess she watches TV," I mumbled. To tell you the truth, back then I didn't care very much about Mrs. Blackert.

But Cara did care.

Sometime during the summer Cara had decided that Mrs. Blackert was a witch. It all started with a thick, black book Cara took from her father's bookshelf. She was always reading his books, especially those she wasn't supposed to read. I don't think Mr. Hadaway even noticed, though. He was usually too immersed in a book himself.

This book really grabbed Cara. For two weeks her eyes were glued to it. It was about magic and the occult, and I guess there were quite a few chapters about witch-craft too, because after she read that book, Cara never stopped talking about witches. She babbled about them day and night, spewing out facts like a fountain.

She told me all sorts of witch trivia. She explained how there are good witches, not just bad witches. "But there aren't too many good ones, Laura. Most of them are rotten to the core," Cara declared, and believe it or not, she was serious.

She told me that unlike vampires, witches could

perform their magic during the day *and* night. "The only thing that stops them," she said, "are eclipses of the moon and the sun, which don't happen all that often."

Everything I said and did reminded Cara of witches. One day while I was slathering myself with suntan lotion, Cara started describing how witches smear flying ointment over their bodies before flying off to witches' meetings, or "sabbats," as she called them.

"That's just what I needed to hear," I told her, grimacing at my greasy limbs.

When I mentioned that Jan and Eliza, two of my other friends, no longer wanted to hang around with her because they were sick and tired of hearing about witches, she ignored me completely.

Instead, she said, "Did you know, Laura, that witches always gather in groups of thirteen, because thirteen is said to be an evil number?"

Each morning while I went to tennis clinic, Cara went to the library to read some more about witches. Every afternoon she filled me in on what she'd read. By the end of the summer, despite myself, I was something of a witch expert too.

Old Mrs. Blackert

I suppose if there was anyone in Dove's Cove who Cara was going to single out as a witch, it had to be old Mrs.

Blackert. She was very mysterious. No one ever saw her. I bet there wasn't one person on our entire block who could even describe what she looked like. Mrs. Blackert never came to any neighborhood functions. She never slurped punch or munched on pigs in a blanket at the annual block party. She never stood around the bonfire belting out carols at the neighborhood Christmas pageant. To most people she was probably nothing more than a shadow hovering in a dusky window or, even more rarely, a black silhouette hurrying down a darkened street.

Also, she lived in a sinister old house.

I think it was the ivy that made her house look so spooky. If it hadn't been for that dark-green ivy slithering up those walls, Mrs. Blackert's house would've been your average, run-of-the-mill, big old house. If not for that ivy, you'd have said it was just an unkempt gray stucco with a red door and a matching red-slate roof. Instead, it was the kind of house that made you think twice about ringing the doorbell. It was shadowy and gloomy, and I'm sure it was because of the ivy that drooped over the dark, watchful windows, clung to the chipped gray paint, coiled around the gutters, and twisted about the chimney. Tendrils of ivy were even wound about the dark, gnarly trees in Mrs. Blackert's front yard. In my opinion it was trying to take over the house.

15

Orange Cats

It was Wednesday.

Although it was hot outside, the sky was full of sagging, purple clouds that looked so low, I half expected them to plop out of the heavens.

Cara and I were walking Nimbo. Cara said that he needed a new activity besides lying around all day in a dirt hole. I guess he stayed in that earthen cave because it was nice and cool, but I didn't tell this to Cara. I didn't want to sound like a know-it-all when I hardly knew a thing about animals.

We turned onto my block, and I noticed that a couple of boys were on the street playing with a Frisbee. All at once my heart started going haywire. I knew they wouldn't bother me, but I was still afraid of them. Fear was a feeling that, like my shadow, I couldn't seem to shake.

We were almost in front of my house when a flash of orange whizzed by us, darting under a hedge. Seeing it, Nimbo lifted his scruffy brown head, sniffed the thick, wet air, and then wearily dropped his nose back to the ground.

"It's one of those cats!" Cara cried, pointing at the rustling green hedge. "It's one of Mrs. Blackert's orange cats! Why do you think she has all those cats, Laura?"

I knew then that Cara wasn't going to leave poor Mrs. Blackert alone. Sometimes she got these weird notions into her head that she simply wouldn't give up.

"What about all those hissing orange creatures, huh?" Another thing about Cara is that she was always saying "huh." I think she said it so that you'd have to respond with a word, a shrug, a shake of your head, anything to show her that you were listening.

I shrugged.

"All orange. Why orange, Laura? Why not black, gray, or white? And there are so many of them. There must be thousands! Every time I turn around, there's an orange cat behind me. It's like they're stalking me or something!" Cara shook her head. Her glasses slid down her nose. It was hot and humid outside. Cara's nose was like an oily slide.

We paused to let Nimbo squirt on a twig. It was very slow going with Nimbo because of his arthritis and his ever-lifting leg. While Nimbo did his thing for about the hundredth time, I thought about Mrs. Blackert's crazy orange cats. There *were* a lot of them, not a thousand, but about a dozen or so. It was kind of strange, the way they were all orange—a strange red orange, the color of wet rust. When the weather was cold, I never saw them, but as soon as it turned warm, they were crawling all over the neighborhood. I'd see them hanging from trees, dangling from fences, and running across the street. Sometimes, when I was lying in my backyard, I'd catch one staring at me, studying me carefully with its pale-green eyes.

But Mrs. Blackert's orange cats didn't really bother me, and the fact that she had them didn't, in my opinion, make her a witch.

"Maybe Mrs. Blackert likes animals," I suggested as we resumed our painfully slow walk. I thought this sounded pretty reasonable.

"PLEASE! Likes animals my foot!" snapped Cara.

"What about your foot?" I asked bitingly. It drives me crazy when people say things that don't make sense.

"Come on, Laura!" Cara rolled her eyes. "Those cats are her *familiars*." I knew this was one of the zany terms she'd picked up from her witch books. "They're her *imps*," Cara continued, "the creatures who do her dirty work. All witches have them. Some have rats, but most have cats."

"Well," I said, "it's nice to know that most witches have good taste." I'd take a cat over a rat any day. Rats really gross me out.

"Besides," she said, ignoring me, "if Mrs. Blackert is such an animal lover, why doesn't she have any dogs? Huh?" We both stared at Nimbo. He stopped dead in his tracks and stared back. He was brown and white with a stubby tail and long ears with curly hair on them. His eyes had a strange, marbly glow. Cara said that this was because the poor old guy had cataracts.

Finally I just shrugged. It was possible that Mrs. Blackert didn't like dogs. The world is full of people who, for whatever reason, don't like certain animals. Take my mother, for instance. She didn't like *any* animals. She wouldn't even let me have a goldfish!

"That old hag doesn't have any dogs," Cara said, answering her own question, "because dogs don't like witches! Nimbo won't go anywhere near her scary old house!"

Now this latter bit of information didn't exactly surprise me; as this walk was proving, Nimbo wasn't all that enthusiastic about going anywhere. I bet if we'd given him a choice, he would've just stayed in his earthen cave.

It seemed to me that Cara was making a big deal out of nothing. Why shouldn't Mrs. Blackert have cats? They're easy. Give them food and a litter box and they're happy. Dogs are hard—you have to walk, play with, and clean up after them.

I guess Cara saw the skeptical look on my face, because she smirked at me. It was her "I know something you don't know" look.

"What?" I asked.

Cara smirked again, more broadly this time. She was a good smirker, Cara, she really was. She not only smirked with her mouth, like most people, but she also threw in one eye for good measure, scrunching and squeezing it till it looked like a crumpled flower petal.

"I hate to tell you this, Laura," she said, though I knew she loved telling me, "but Mrs. Blackert isn't your typical old lady."

We were a couple of yards away from Mrs. Blackert's house when the paperboy, Greg Mox, came barreling down the sidewalk on his bike, tossing papers this way and that. Mox was a rangy guy with shaggy orange hair and so many freckles, it looked as though someone had sprinkled paprika all over his skin. Because of his freckles Cara nicknamed him Mox Pox, which, not surprisingly, he hated.

Anyway, when Mox saw us, he sneered.

I'm not sure whether Nimbo was reacting to Mox's nasty face or the nearness of Mrs. Blackert's house, but all of a sudden he yelped. His yelp started off high, like a scream, and ended in a sort of wolfish howl. When he was through, Nimbo tucked his stubby tail between his legs and started pulling us toward Cara's cottage. It was the most energetic thing I'd seen him do all summer.

Behind us Greg Mox began to laugh like a crazy man. His laugh reminded me of the neigh of a horse—it was loud and obvious, and you could tell he was making fun of us. All of a sudden the boys in the street stopped playing Frisbee. They stood staring at us, wondering, I supposed, whether they should laugh too.

But before they could do a thing, Cara whirled around and said to Mox, "Got a problem, Mox Pox?" She hurled her voice at him as if it were a stone.

Casually, as if he didn't hear her, Mox looked the other way. But I knew he'd heard her all right, because all of a sudden his laughter faded, his bike spun around, and he rode off in the opposite direction.

Saved, I thought, as the boys resumed their game.

We were a few houses away from the cottage when the dark, swollen sky burst, dousing us with warm August rain.

Cara's Research

On Thursday it was once again sunny as well as hot. Cara and I were lying next to the pool in my backyard, basking in the late-afternoon sun. I was worn out. I'd played tennis all morning with this bag of bones from my school named Mary Jane Benzer. Mary Jane had these unbelievably long arms—monkey arms, Cara called them—which made her a terrific tennis player. On Saturday we were to play against each other for the team trophy. Today the coach had made us play a practice match, which, following a grueling tiebreaker, I'd won.

After the match Mary Jane said to me, "I'll get you yet, Laura"; then she whacked me in the butt with the racket and laughed, an awful, snuffly laugh.

My mother, who was terrifically chummy with Mrs. Benzer, was constantly asking me why I wasn't friendlier with Mary Jane. "But, Laura," she urged, "you go to the same school; you're in the same grade and on the same tennis team. And she's such a nice girl. Good upbringing."

Time and again I explained to my mother that Mary Jane Benzer was the biggest nerd in my class. When she wasn't bragging about how great she is in tennis, she was droning on about her boring old soap operas. Mary Jane was simply obsessed with the soaps.

"And she's not even a nice nerd," my friend Eliza had said. Which was true. Mary Jane could actually get pretty nasty if you teased her enough.

My mother just didn't get the picture. I supposed she was too old to understand, so after a while I just quit explaining it.

Still, nerd or not, I had to admit that Mary Jane was a pretty super tennis player. She could really hit a tennis ball. She'd had me running all over the court.

Though I could barely move, Cara was bursting with energy. She couldn't sit still. She kept flopping around in her lounge chair like a big, slimy fish.

Finally she let out this long, noisy sigh and said, "As

long as I've lived in Dove's Cove, I've had a funny feeling about old Mrs. Blackert. Every time I walk by her house, I get the heebie-jeebies. Don't you?"

I shook my head. I didn't get any weird feelings when I walked by Mrs. Blackert's house—not back then, anyway.

"Today, while you were playing tennis," said Cara, ignoring my response, "I went to the library."

What else is new? I thought.

"I flipped through old newspapers looking for stories about the Blackerts. I thought that maybe I'd find something unusual. And I did! That's what I was doing while you were concentrating on a stupid green ball!"

Cara didn't like tennis, probably because she wasn't very good at it. Once during the summer I tried to play tennis with her. But each time the ball came her way, she acted as though it were a grenade. She hunched her shoulders and froze, so that the ball either smashed her in the head or bounced off her shoulder.

Beside me Cara twiddled her tanned toes and said, "Today I learned that the Blackerts came from England. You may not know this, Laura, but England has always been full of witches."

I didn't know it, but I didn't like her assuming I didn't know it. She was always assuming I didn't know things, which made me feel kind of stupid.

"During the seventeenth century there were so many

witches in England that this witch finder started hunting them down. He found witches everywhere, even in the royal court. I bet a lot of those English witches sailed here, to America, just to get away from that guy. It wasn't long after he started hunting them that witches turned up in Massachusetts."

"But . . . " I wanted to tell Cara that it had never been proven that all those women who were accused of being witches really were witches, but Cara cut me off. She didn't like anyone to interrupt her stories. She was on a roll, and when she was rolling, there was just no stopping her.

Cara leaped off her lounge chair and walked over to my mother's roses. She ran a finger around the rim of a pale-pink one, sending three of its petals fluttering to the ground. She picked up one of the fallen petals, stuck it on her nose, and said, "The Blackerts settled in Massachusetts. I bet that wasn't a coincidence. I bet they wanted to be with their *own kind*." Cara cocked her head at me and raised her brows for dramatic effect.

"They settled in a town called Brigham, near the sea. There were thirteen of them. *Thirteen,* Laura, twelve sisters and their mother. No father. Supposedly the Blackert women were beautiful. They all had pale-white, powdery skin and red hair. Flaming red, like fire."

Despite myself, I was getting interested in her story.

A Barnacle

Cara sat down at the edge of my chair. The rose petal was still stuck to her nose. It made her look goofy. I wondered if she even remembered it was there.

"There was this one nosy reporter in Brigham who took a special interest in the Blackerts. His name was Carl Hilb. He worked for a paper called the *Brigham Barnacle*. Do you know what a barnacle is, Laura?"

I shook my head. Barnacle—it was one of those words I thought I knew until someone asked me to explain it.

Cara, though, had a great vocabulary. Sometimes I wondered if she spent her evenings memorizing the entire dictionary. She said, "A barnacle is a little shellfish that attaches itself to things like boat bottoms and rocks. When someone is a barnacle, they're clingy, they hang on you. Carl Hilb was a barnacle when it came to the Blackerts. He spied on them and wrote nasty articles in his newspaper column."

"Why?" I asked. To me the guy sounded like a real pest.

Cara furrowed her brow. She swatted her nose, launching the rose petal into the air. She watched, surprised, as it glided to the ground.

For a moment I thought I'd thrown her off a bit with my question. But then she said, "I think Hilb hounded the Blackerts because he sensed there was something odd about them. Later, he was convinced that they were witches."

I took a sip of lemonade and crunched noisily on the ice.

"Go on," I said.

"The Blackerts brought paintings with them from England. Portraits. Unusual portraits. The Blackerts started selling these paintings, and people came from miles away just to see them. Supposedly the eyes of the portraits shifted and winked. The portraits' expressions changed—as though they were *alive*!"

I shuddered. I certainly wouldn't want my mother to hang a portrait like that in our house.

"It seems that the Blackerts had painted those portraits in England. They began painting people in Brigham too. They had their subjects sit for them for about an hour, then they asked them for anything personal, like a tie, a hat, or a stocking. They claimed that these articles helped them finish their portraits. Weird, huh?"

It was weird, but it wasn't *that* weird. I mean, aren't all painters eccentric? Last year our art teacher told us about a famous painter named van Gogh who cut off his own ear! Now *that's* weird!

"Kind of," I said. I was uncomfortably hot, and dying to go for a swim, but I wanted to hear what else Cara had to say. Though she hadn't yet told me anything truly remarkable, I had a feeling she was building up to something big.

Cara wiped her sweaty nose and pushed up her glasses. They were intellectual glasses, round with thin gold frames.

"Well, Carl Hilb wrote in his column that there was something sinister about the Blackerts and their paintings. But instead of scaring people off, his claims only made them want those paintings more." Cara got up and started to pace the lawn. She continued, "Strange things began happening in Brigham, Laura. People disappeared. They vanished without a trace. But no one really cared too much, because the people who vanished were losers, zeros. They were crooks and grouches. No one missed them. Except that reporter guy, Carl Hilb. He maintained that all the people who disappeared had one thing in common: They'd all had their portraits painted by the Blackerts!"

Back then I didn't take what Cara was telling me too seriously, so I said something I'd never say now. I said, "Hey, why don't we get Mrs. Blackert to do a portrait of Lucy!" That was one way to stop my sister from hogging the phone and barging into my room!

But Cara didn't laugh. She stopped pacing and glared at me. "Not funny, Laura," she responded—and oh, how right she was! "Do you want to hear what happened or not?"

"I do."

"Still no one in Brigham listened to Hilb. Finally, in his newspaper column, he accused the Blackerts of being witches. He wrote that they'd been blamed for a bunch of mysterious disappearances in England. He claimed that they'd been forced out of the country." Once again Cara sat down at the edge of my lounge chair.

"Do you think he made that up?"

"No, Laura, I don't," Cara replied, "because the day after that column appeared, Hilb disappeared! When he stopped showing up for work, his boss, the editor of the *Brigham Barnacle*, got worried. He went to Hilb's rooming house. All of Hilb's things were there, all of his clothes, everything, but not Hilb."

Everything has a reasonable explanation, doesn't it? That's what my mother told us, and that's how I thought back then, so I said, "Cara, people disappear all the time." I was thinking of milk cartons and how there's always a new face on them. I used to wonder where those kids were. Now that I've given up rational thinking, I wonder if any of them ended up like Cara.

"Maybe they do," Cara admitted. She took her glasses off and wiped them on my towel. Putting them back on, she said, "I haven't even told you the really wild part of this story, Laura. Shortly after Hilb vanished, the Blackerts gave a painting of him to his old mother. Everyone in Brigham thought this was a very nice gesture. But not Old Lady Hilb. She didn't keep the portrait. She donated it to the town museum. She insisted the portrait gave her the creeps—that Carl was always watching her, that he made faces, that he spoke to her."

"Did anyone else see him make faces?"

"I guess not. Everyone said Old Lady Hilb was nuts."

"She probably was," I said.

"Come on, Laura, don't you think it's strange that Hilb disappeared right after he wrote that article about the Blackerts? Don't you think that they used a spell to punish him?"

"I don't know," I replied truthfully. "Did you read anything else?"

"Nah," uttered Cara. Her dark hair was wet and stringy with sweat. "That's all I had time for."

Just then we heard a loud rustling sound, and we both jumped.

A Dip in the Pool

I saw one of Mrs. Blackert's orange cats stroll out of the bushes, its long, red-tipped tail twirling around in the air. It was a fat cat, and it strode proudly back and forth on our patio, staring at us over its shoulder.

"Look," I murmured to Cara, pointing. As soon as I

said it, I realized I'd made a mistake. After she read that crazy witch book, Cara stopped liking cats. When she saw the orange cat, she leaped to her feet and chased after it. Cara was very quick. She grabbed that poor cat by its long orange tail and threw it into the pool. As it flew through the air, it wailed, a high, long baby cry. The cat landed in the pool with a great splash and flailed about.

I didn't waste a second. I jumped into the pool, pulled the cat out of the water, and placed it gently on the grass.

The cat shook itself, then turned around slowly, opened its mouth, and hissed at Cara. Before I could blink, it was gone.

"Why'd you do that?" Cara asked me. "What a vicious cat!"

"I'd be nasty too if you threw me into the pool," I said, drying myself.

And that's exactly what she did.

Mrs. O

The next day, Friday, our housekeeper, Mrs. Omeyer, who we called Mrs. O for short, picked me up from tennis clinic. My father, the lawyer, was at work. My mother was showing a house. She worked as a real estate agent in Dove's Cove. For a long time she'd been moaning that business was terrible. "I've shown the same house ten times," she grumbled during the spring.

But over the summer things had picked up. All of a sudden everyone wanted to buy a house.

While Mrs. O drove home, I described our big tournament, which was tomorrow. I explained that the trophy was mine if I beat Mary Jane Benzer.

Mrs. O, who was definitely one of my biggest fans, said, "Go get her, Laura."

When we neared our house, I saw Cara sitting on the curb waiting for me. She was dressed in cutoff jeans and a boy's white undershirt.

"What's wrong with that girl? She always looks like a hobo," Mrs. O groused, wrinkling her nose. Mrs. O was a pudgy woman with a slick, neat bun of steely hair. She'd been with us for years, and not once during all those years had I ever seen one strand of her hair out of place. Cara said that Mrs. O's hair was probably fake, that it was probably pasted to her head.

"I bet that every night she peels off that hair of hers and hangs it on her bedpost," Cara told me.

Though I liked Mrs. O, I thought that maybe Cara was right.

Mrs. O had small features: tiny twinkling eyes, a skinny little nose, which stuck up straight in the air so that you always had a good view of her nostrils, and small, pursed lips. I was sure my mother liked her because they both had the same clean, starched, no-nonsense look.

Mrs. O liked Jan and Eliza, but she wasn't too crazy about Cara. She believed that Cara was a bad influence on me, that Cara was "too smart for her britches."

When I got out of the car, Cara strolled toward me. She laughed at my tennis whites. I have to wear them; otherwise I'm not allowed on the court.

"Ah, come on," I said. I gazed longingly at Cara's cut-off jeans. They had a soft white fringe on the bottom. Earlier in the summer I had cut a pair of my jeans into shorts and Mrs. O had found them. She held them up with two fingers, as though they were radioactive, and marched off to show them to my mother. My mother had a fit. She came after me, waving the jean shorts around in the air. She launched into this long, boring lecture about how she spends all this money on clothes to make me look nice, while I insist upon dressing like a ragamuffin. Then, to my horror, she stuffed the jean shorts into the garbage can with a bunch of eggshells and coffee grounds.

"Guess where I was this morning," Cara demanded. She had a funny gleam in her eyes. I knew then that I hadn't heard the last of Mrs. Blackert.

"At the library," I ventured. I mean, where else would she be?

"Yup," she said smugly, "and have I got a story for you!"

Mrs. Blackert's Missing Husband

When we were sitting at the patio table with two big glasses of lemonade and some fat turkey sandwiches, compliments of Mrs. O, Cara began to talk.

"I did some more reading," Cara said between bites, "about Mrs. Blackert."

I glanced uneasily at Mrs. Blackert's place. I couldn't see much, only the red roof of her house and her hedges. Still, I had this eerie feeling that she was listening in on us.

"Do you know the story about her husband?" Cara asked me.

"No," I said. There was a very peaceful and comforting time in my life when I knew very little about Mrs. Blackert.

Cara shoved the last of her sandwich into her mouth and said in a muffled voice, "Mrs. Blackert's husband fell off the face of the earth, just like that reporter guy, Hilb."

I must stop here and tell you that Cara had this disgusting habit of speaking with food in her mouth. Sometimes wet globs shot past her lips and slapped me in the face, which drove me crazy. I mean, why couldn't she chew and swallow *before* she spoke? More than once I was tempted to give her this boring book my mother made me read about manners. I figured I'd highlight the part about eating, but I never gave it to her. It'd just be a waste of time. Cara would laugh at me. She didn't care about things like manners. When she had something to say, she just came right out and said it. No matter what. And the truth was that despite myself I liked her for it. It made her kind of different and exciting.

"Tell me the story," I said, looking at my sandwich.

"Here, read about it yourself." Cara reached into the back pocket of her jean shorts and pulled out a couple of crumpled papers. She smoothed them and pushed them across the table. They were copies of articles from our gossipy town newspaper, *Dove's Cove Doings*.

The first article was titled "Doug Hirst III Marries."

"Who's Doug Hirst the Third?" I asked Cara. Though the name sounded vaguely familiar, I couldn't quite place it.

"Boy, are you thick, Laura! Doug Hirst, as in Hirst Street. As in the fanciest street in all of Dove's Cove. As in Mrs. Blackert's husband!"

"Oh," I mumbled. Of course. Silly me. The Hirsts. Everyone knew them. They were such a big deal in Dove's Cove that a street had been named after them. But I hadn't known that Mrs. Blackert had married one of them! Come to think of it, even though she was a Mrs., I never thought of her as being married.

I was going to ask Cara why, if Mrs. Blackert and Doug Hirst were husband and wife, they didn't share the same last name, but Cara anticipated my question. She was almost always a good step ahead of me.

She said, "Mrs. Blackert kept her own name when she got married. Maybe witches are feminists or something, who knows? All I know is that the Hirsts hated her for that. *Read the article, Laura.*"

I forgot all about my half-eaten turkey sandwich. I read:

> A lot of hearts will give a great sigh this October when the most desirable bachelor in Dove's Cove, Doug Hirst III, weds Brigham, Massachusetts, resident Adele Blackert. Though Hirst is one of the oldest and most respected names in the county, Adele Blackert, who immigrated from a small county in England with her mother and eleven sisters, is not taking the Hirst name. . . .

The article went on to discuss, in a rather snotty way, how the Blackert sisters and their mother wanted nothing to do with the marriage. They would neither attend the wedding nor pay for it. They didn't like big-shot Doug Hirst III. All the Blackerts, with the exception of

Adele, my nutty neighbor, thought he was a slime. Clearly the author of the article didn't agree with them and thought the Blackerts were a bunch of lunatics for not idolizing the guy.

In case you haven't already guessed, *Dove's Cove Doings* always sympathized with the rich and famous.

"Read the next one," Cara said, pointing to another article.

This one was titled "Doug Hirst III Mysteriously Vanishes."

This one looked good. I read:

> Doug Hirst III was reported missing by his long-time friend and business partner, Brad Deever, who became worried when Hirst did not show up for work.
>
> Deever told police: "Two days go by and Dougie doesn't show up at the office. I get a little worried. Actually, I'm ticked off. I'm thinking that maybe old Dougie boy is playing hooky, you know—gambling and whooping it up— while I'm working my bones off. Wouldn't be the first time. . . .
>
> "So I call Adele, his wife, to ask her if old Dougie boy is home. She says yes, he is. This really gets me ticked off. I mean, what's he doing home when we have a business to run? So I

ask Adele what he's doing, and she says the weirdest thing: 'He's hanging around.' Then she bursts out laughing. She just loses it on the phone. I always told Dougie that you had to watch those redheads. Yes sirree. Red hair is nice and all, don't get me wrong, but it does something to the brain. I'm sure of it.

"So I hang up the phone and drive my Jag over to Dougie's place. I figure I'll have it out with him, you know? Give him a good chunk of my mind.

"I knock on the door and Adele answers, looking mighty fine, as usual. I say, 'I'd like to have a word with Dougie.' I'm all smiles because I'm trying to be cool and hold my temper.

"She says, 'Sure. Come inside.' She's as sweet as cherry pie. She takes me into the dining room, and I see there's a new painting there. It's a portrait of old Dougie boy. Pretty good too. Real lifelike.

"I say to Adele, 'Did you do that?' Because I know she paints.

"She says, 'Yes.'

"I tell her that it's a good likeness and all, then I tell her again that I want to have a word with old Dougie boy.

"She says, 'Go right ahead.' Then she just

stands there, those white arms of hers crossed, her black eyes watching me.

"I'm a little confused, so I say, 'Well, where is he?'

"That's when she says the queerest thing of all. 'He's right there!' She points to Dougie's portrait. That's when I get it. She wants me to talk to the painting!

"I try to calm down, but it's not easy. No sirree. My blood pressure is going nuts, and it feels like my head is going to blow up. I say, all slow and calm like, 'Adele, I need to speak to the real Doug Hirst.' I'm not sure how else to put it.

"She says, 'That is the real Doug Hirst!' She says it like I'm some kind of a moron.

"That's when I get out of there. What else is there to say? Clearly, she's flipped her lid!"

The article went on to say that Mrs. Blackert was a suspect in her husband's disappearance. Apparently, there were rumors that the two of them hadn't been getting along.

I looked up to find Cara shoving the rest of my sandwich into her mouth. I didn't say anything. I just let her have it. Lately she was always hungry. That's because her father had suddenly turned macrobiotic. Cara said that now he ate only these strange little beans and grains he bought in a health-food store, and when he cooked that stuff, it all tasted the same—like a paper bag. She said she was slowly starving.

I was lucky. Mrs. O was a terrific cook.

Cara looked at me guiltily, then handed me another article. She probably had a whole newspaper's worth of clippings stuffed into the pockets of her jean shorts. This article said that the police eventually dropped the case. They let Mrs. Blackert off the hook. Neither they nor the FBI, nor a private investigator hired by the Hirsts, could find any evidence against her. Mrs. Blackert just kept telling them all the same story—that her husband, Doug Hirst III, was hanging on her dining-room wall.

Great, I thought, I have a basket case for a neighbor!

"What do you think happened to this guy?" I asked Cara. I knew she had a theory. She always had a theory.

"I think that old witch Mrs. Blackert put a spell on him. I think she made him disappear the same way that she, or her family, made Carl Hilb disappear, the same way they made all those other people in Massachusetts disappear!"

I thought about this for a minute. I saw the common thread, the paintings and the vanishings, but it sounded very far-fetched to me.

Ghost Stories

That night Cara came over after dinner. We were going to sit in my backyard and tell each other ghost stories. As I briefly mentioned earlier, storytelling was one thing we both loved. It was a unique and important part of our friendship. It was something I couldn't do with any of my other friends, because no one was as imaginative as Cara.

"Where are you going now?" my mother asked me, though it was pretty obvious that I was headed for the side door.

"Out."

"Laura, do you think that's wise? Don't you think you should go to sleep early? You have the tournament tomorrow."

I shrugged. In case you haven't noticed, I shrug a lot. Believe it or not, you can say a lot with a little bounce of your shoulders. With that particular shrug I was saying that I *had* to go out. That night the moon was full. Cara and I believed that there was something spectacular about a big, white, ghostly moon. We believed it made us more creative. When the moon was full, our stories were extra creepy.

"You'll be sorry tomorrow, Laura. I'm sure Mary Jane Benzer is already in bed." My mother shook her head. It's funny—I was always shrugging, and my mother was always shaking her head. I watched her yellow hair swing back and forth, and then I opened the door and went outside.

I heard Lucy say to my mother, "She's crazy, and so is that girl Cara. Two crazy ghouls, that's what they are!" I laughed, because I think our stories scared her. A few nights that summer, while waiting for a boy to come and pick her up, she'd sat outside with us and brushed her long, silky hair and listened to our stories for a while. But at some point my sister always got up and left. She never sat through a full story.

When I was outside, I looked up at the moon. It was perfectly round and white, and so big, it looked as though I could reach out and pull it down from the sky.

"Nice, huh?" Cara said. Her face was tilted upward, toward the moon.

"It is," I agreed.

You might be wondering why, since Cara had a graveyard in back of her cottage, we didn't go there. With that old chiming church and moonglow falling like white mist over the tombstones, it seems like the perfect setting for ghost stories. But Cara argued that her yard was too overgrown to sit in and that it was swarming with bugs, skunks, and rabid raccoons.

"You never know what'll come creeping out of those grass stalks, Laura," she told me.

She did have a point. Her backyard was rather wild.

41

Her father liked it that way. He didn't believe in mowing. He insisted it destroyed wildlife. Still, I thought her reason was merely an excuse. Though she wouldn't admit it, I was pretty sure she was as scared of that graveyard as was I.

We sat down at the patio table. I lit a little citronella candle and put it between us. The wick sizzled and spat, and then a citrus smell wafted into the warm night air.

Cara and I took our ghost stories very seriously.

We were always trying to outdo each other. Between us there was a secret competition to see whose story was the scariest. My stories were usually about vampires. I could start out talking about a witch or a werewolf, but somehow a vampire always crept its way into my tale and took over. To me vampires were very romantic.

Until that summer Cara's stories had always been unpredictable. She used to make up all kinds of monsters: seaweed creatures, killer snowmen, giant worms, you name it. After she read the witch book, though, all of Cara's stories were about witches. But even when I knew that, I was never sure what was coming next. The only thing I did know for sure was that the endings wouldn't be happy. Cara said happy endings were a copout.

"It's my turn to go first," Cara announced. "You went first last time."

"Okay." I was glad, since it gave me some time to think up a tale.

"Tonight," said Cara, with a mischievous twinkle in her eyes, "I'm going to do something a little bit different. A bit unconventional." She looked at me, then licked her finger and flicked it swiftly through the flame of the candle, which was something I could never bring myself to do. Cara claimed it didn't hurt if you did it fast enough.

"Uh-oh," I moaned, watching her unhappily. I didn't like it when Cara used the words "different" and "unconventional." Sometimes she had very peculiar ideas.

"Tonight, Laura, we're going on a witch hunt!"

I opened my mouth to protest, but Cara held up her hand. "Shhh," she whispered. "We're going to spy on old Mrs. Blackert!"

"No way!" I exclaimed, cold waves of terror washing over me.

"What are you, *scared?*" Cara asked me with her trademark smirk. She flicked her finger three more times through the wavering flame.

I should tell you that this "are you scared?" business was a clever tactic Cara used to get me to do things I didn't want to do. It was a taunt, a challenge, and it always worked. I'd never admit that I was afraid, not to her anyway. She knew that I wanted to seem tough, even if I wasn't.

"I'm not scared!" I lied. "I just don't think it's nice to spy on an old lady!"

"Old lady my foot!" snapped Cara. "Mean old witch is more like it! Come on, Laura, don't be a *sissy*."

It was being called a sissy that made me do it.

It was like a slap in the face, because it was the truth. I was a wimp, a yellow belly. Ashamed, I followed Cara into Mrs. Blackert's yard.

Creeping and Crawling

All around Mrs. Blackert's yard, like a big, green, prickly fence, were these enormous evergreen hedges. Cara called them "the monster hedges" because they were unusually tall.

As I neared those hedges, I imagined I felt the moon shining on my back, and it didn't feel warm. It felt cold, icy, as though a glacier were pressing into my skin. It made me shiver, a deep shiver that rattled my bones and sent ripples up and down my spine.

It seemed to me too, as I crawled through the hedges on my hands and knees, that they were alive. Their needles bit into my skin and their branches felt like cat claws—long, sharp, grabbing claws. They scraped my neck and ripped through my hair. Branches curled around my ankles and yanked at my arms, trying to hold me back. At one point, in order to untangle myself, I had to pull a clump of my hair from one of the limbs and the hair broke, leaving behind a big, yellow, messy ball.

After a lot of scratching and crawling, we were in Mrs. Blackert's yard, standing very still, breathing hard.

I looked around. My mother kept our grounds very neat—manicured, she called it—so that not even a weed was out of place, but Mrs. Blackert's yard was a jungle. Big bushes loomed in the shadows; I couldn't tell where one started and another finished. To me those misshapen bushes looked like animals, crouched and ready to pounce. I thought that I could hear them growling softly, making low, rumbling sounds deep in their throats, but then I stuffed my fingers into my ears and told myself to stop thinking crazy thoughts.

Gigantic weeds grew everywhere. They soared out of the ivy, which carpeted the ground. Some of them came up to my shoulder, most of them reached my waist. All the trees were black and bent and sickly. They sort of leaned into one another, their branches intertwined. All in all, the place was a mess.

I'd just noticed what looked like a greenhouse, attached to the back of the main house, when Cara tugged at my arm.

"Come on," she whispered, tiptoeing ahead of me. I followed. It was better than going back through those awful hedges.

We crept to the greenhouse, rounded it, then inched

our way around that big house looking for a lighted window. Most of the windows were dark. It seemed to me that the house was empty, and that I'd soon be able to go home, climb into my bed, and nestle under the covers like good old Mary Jane Benzer, when Cara cried softly, "Look!"

I groaned.

Directly above us was a window. It was open. Out of it poured soft, golden light. The light was wavy—it grew and shrank and flickered, like candlelight.

"It's too high," I said hopefully. The way I figured it, it'd take almost two of me to be able to see into that window.

Cara looked around, then smiled.

"Be right back," she whispered. She hiked away from me, through the weeds and tangles of ivy, toward an old metal garbage can.

I stood perfectly still underneath the window.

I was certain that if I turned my head and raised my eyes just a fraction, they'd meet the flaming red demon eyes of Mrs. Blackert. I was sure that while I stared straight ahead, frozen like a soldier, her horrible green face was bearing down on me. I pictured her long, skinny, black tongue slithering its way hungrily across her eager gray lips. I was so scared that my eyes began to water. I blinked desperately, hoping that Cara wouldn't notice. She'd think I was crying. She'd know I was scared.

I prayed that she'd be very quiet carrying that old metal can.

While I was standing there waiting for Cara, I saw a flash of lightning. Then I heard it, a soft, low, rolling sound—thunder. I gazed up and saw clouds, like long gray ghosts, gathering in the sky, blocking out the moon.

"Cool!" Cara said when it thundered again. She placed the garbage can against the house, upside down.

"Cool?" I exclaimed. To me it was anything but cool. "We could be killed, struck by lightning!"

"Shh," hissed Cara. "Come on!" She climbed atop the garbage can and peered into the window.

Mrs. Blackert's Dining Room

I should tell you that I didn't climb onto the garbage can right away. For a minute or two I stood with my feet firmly planted on the ground, trying to talk some sense into myself. My sensible, reasonable side, which sounded a lot like my mother, told me to get out of there right away. It told me to go home and crawl under the covers. It was persuasive, it really was, but in the end my curious side won out. When I heard Cara whisper, "Wow," I scrambled onto the garbage can too.

Despite myself, I really did want to know what was inside that colossal old house.

Lightning flashed and the can wobbled, and for a moment I was certain we'd both topple over with a big crash, but we clutched the ivy on the windowsill and the can steadied.

Thunder grumbled behind us. It sounded closer.

I looked into the room. About a thousand tall black candles blazed in candelabras. A breeze swept through the air, causing the candle flames to dip and dance. The effect was eerie, magical, and altogether dazzling.

The room was a formal and majestic dining room, something that looked like it belonged in an old English castle. Thick red-velvet curtains framed the windows, and hundreds of portraits surrounded by heavy gold frames covered the walls.

It didn't take me long to figure out that there was something peculiar about those portraits. They looked like more than oil paints on canvas. They looked real. Too real. Though they made me uneasy, I stared at them. I was almost certain I saw the eyes in the paintings shift and slide, but then I blinked hard and told myself that it had to be a trick of the flickering candles. Still, I couldn't shake this awful feeling that at any minute the people in those portraits would thrust out their hands, grab the sides of the picture frames, and drag themselves into the dining room.

In the middle of the room, on a mostly red oriental carpet, stood an enormous table. The table was set. It was a strange setting. Little white bowls sat in front of each chair, but there were no napkins or silverware, and more black candles burned in the middle of the table. Also on the table were a gold hand mirror, a little jar, and a tiny silver spoon.

Mrs. Blackert

Suddenly a woman swept into the room. She walked swiftly toward us. At the same time a flash of bright white lightning lit up the night. I crouched, afraid that in the brilliant light she'd see me, and I dragged Cara down with me. I guess I moved too fast, because the garbage can gave a great rattle and a terrific lurch. I fell backward. I grabbed at the ivy, but it broke in my hands. A second later I lay in the weeds alongside Cara, the wind knocked out of me.

"Idiot," she spat through clenched teeth.

We would've been discovered if it hadn't been for a great crash of thunder that shook the night the very instant the garbage can rattled. I was ready to call it quits then and there, but Cara insisted that we climb back up on the can. I felt like a jerk for making us fall in the first place, and I knew she'd call me a baby if I went home, so very carefully I climbed beside her.

When we gazed into the room again, I gave a little

sigh of relief. The woman, who I assumed was Mrs. Blackert, was standing next to the dining-room table. She was staring intently at the wall and seemed undisturbed. It was clear that she hadn't seen or heard us.

Cara had told me that Mrs. Blackert had to be in her nineties, so I'd always imagined her to be wobbly and wrinkly like an old and forgotten vegetable.

But Mrs. Blackert didn't look old at all. She appeared very nimble and wiry. She didn't dress old either, even though she wore a robe. It was black and silky, with gold embroidery at the neck and sleeves and along the bottom. Her hair was loose. It was no longer red but white, as white as the moon, and long, down to her waist, and wavy. Her face would've blended in with her hair, except that her lips had been colored a dark, dramatic red. Blood red, I thought, staring at them. Her eyes were so black, I wondered if she was wearing eye makeup.

In her own way she was attractive, rather theatrical-looking.

For a moment I wondered if Cara had gotten her dates straight. The woman in that room couldn't possibly be ninety. But Cara was a whiz in everything, including my worst subject—math.

The Ugly Portrait

There was absolutely no one else in the room, but Mrs. Blackert was speaking. When I looked more closely, I saw that she was talking to a portrait on the wall—a portrait of an old, terribly ugly man, so ugly I wondered why anyone had bothered to paint him. He had a few tired, gray hairs on his head, and his skin was yellow and crumbly, like old cheese. His nose was long and thin and pointed, and it twisted to one side of his face, but it was his eyes that were terrifying. They were blue—a watery, diluted blue, and they were small and beady and cold, like a bird's eyes.

Mrs. Blackert was having a chat with this ugly painting. She said, "Today is your birthday, and I must say that you look very lovely this year, dear." Despite my fright, I almost laughed. Was she crazy? That guy in the painting was, by far, the ugliest human being I'd ever seen!

"You should see yourself, all yellow, gray, and hairless. In fact, since it's your one-hundredth birthday, I'll let you see yourself." She spoke with a crisp, clear English accent. Then she clasped her hands together. They were little hands, very white, very pale.

She picked up the gold mirror from the table, and I thought I saw that face in the painting cringe. The mouth seemed to twitch, and the mean little bird eyes seemed to wince, but it was hard to be sure what was real and what wasn't because of all those flickering candles and the lightning, which kept flashing every few minutes. When Mrs. Blackert held the mirror up to the painting, though, I was certain of what I saw. I saw the man in the painting grimace—the thin, sickly lips drooped downward, the lower lip folding over, protruding a bit. After a loud bout of thunder, which almost sent me tumbling to the ground again, I heard the painting moan.

Cara looked at me. Her face was pale; her eyes were as big and round as her glasses. A light rain was falling, causing Cara's glasses to slide down her slick, wet nose. I don't know what I looked like, but I can tell you that my teeth were chattering so hard that a couple of times I chomped on my tongue.

It began raining hard. Thunder crashed directly over our heads. Lightning flashed, one bolt after another, white and blinding in the sky. I waited for it to strike us. They'd told us in school that if we ever got caught outside during a thunderstorm, we should stay away from anything metal, and here I was standing on a garbage can! You can't get any dumber than that!

When I turned once more toward the window, I saw that Mrs. Blackert had put the mirror down. But she was still chatting with that queer painting. Her voice had what Cara would call a lot of inflections, dips, and rises that soared and plunged like a roller coaster.

Mrs. Blackert said to the portrait, "Now, dear, don't get too upset. I know you're vain, but after all, everyone ages. Some just go a little more quickly than others." She laughed and touched her ghostly hair lightly.

Caviar

"To celebrate your birthday, I thought we would have some caviar!" blared Mrs. Blackert. She threw her head back and waved her small white hands around in the air.

I felt as though I was watching an actress in a play. She was very dramatic.

"Yes," she went on, "I suppose you miss that the most. Oh, how you loved caviar!" Her blood-red lips stretched into a taut smile. "Never mind that those horrid little eggs made me gag and break out in bright-red hives. You insisted we eat caviar every night. Never mind that I would have preferred an occasional taco, with cheese and spicy meat." Mrs. Blackert licked her vibrant lips. "But no—black eggs, orange eggs, you fed them to me for breakfast, lunch, and dinner. No, *fed* is not quite right. You *stuffed* them into my mouth with your little silver spoon, laughing while I choked."

I watched Mrs. Blackert reach for the small jar and the little silver spoon on the table. She opened the jar. I grimaced. I knew what it was. It was caviar, those salty black fish eggs. I could spot those eggs anywhere, because I hate them so. It's the texture I don't like. In my mouth those eggs feel like slimy, cold peas. They make me gag. Luckily, no one has ever forced me to eat caviar, and I've never had hives.

While Mrs. Blackert was opening that revolting jar,

cats began pouring into the room. Orange cats. Thirteen of them. They climbed onto the dining-room table, each cat settling itself before a bowl. You'd think that they'd be all over one another and all over Mrs. Blackert, trying to get at those stinky eggs. You'd think that fur would be flying. But the orange cats sat politely while Mrs. Blackert used the little silver spoon to dole out little bits of caviar into each bowl.

While Mrs. Blackert was busy being a good hostess, I looked at the painting. The ugly man's eyes had shifted downward and his eyebrows were all tied up in knots. He was staring at those cats with a terrible, frightening intensity.

"Dinnertime," sang Mrs. Blackert. At exactly the same time the cats bent their heads and lapped up the caviar.

"Happy birthday, dear," Mrs. Blackert chirped to the painting while the cats ate. She looked very satisfied with herself. Meanwhile, in the ugly man's eyes I saw pure, undiluted hatred.

Mrs. Blackert resumed speaking, her voice as slippery and sweet as honey. "Now, dear, I know you never liked cats. You called them fleabags. You said they had an unpleasant odor. As I recall, you killed one once. Drowned my sweet creature—a cat I'd had since my youth. But you must be very lonely in that painting. What kind of wife would I be if I left you all alone on your birthday? No, I couldn't do that. I think you need some warm, furry friends to keep you company tonight!"

Bedtime, Kitties

"Bedtime now, kitties!" Mrs. Blackert said cheerfully. Three times she clapped her hands.

That's when the strangest thing of all happened: I heard a man's voice cry out. It was a pathetic sound, a strangled, gurgling noise that sounded like "No!" I glanced quickly at the painting on the wall. Sure enough, the ugly man's chalky lips were shaped into a perfectly oval O. Then I heard a scuffling noise. I turned my head just in time to see one of the orange cats leap off the dining-room table and hurtle through the air toward the portrait of the ugly man. I thought for sure that its claws would rip through the oil canvas. But that's not what happened! *The cat dove into the painting.* It settled itself on top of the ugly man's yellow head.

The ugly man stayed motionless, a bright-orange lump on his head, a long furry tail dangling past his left eye, a truly awful expression on his face.

Suddenly the other cats jumped into the portrait one by one and arranged themselves about the ugly man.

All but one.

One cat still sat on the dining-room table. It was

staring at Cara. It was the fat cat, the one with the red-tipped tail, the one that Cara had thrown into the pool. I was almost certain I saw yellow flames in its pale eyes.

"What's the matter, my sweet little Felix?" Mrs. Blackert asked this cat.

Sweet little Felix didn't answer her. Instead, he rose up on his legs, scrunched up his back, raised his tail, opened his toothy mouth, and let out a loud, angry hiss. Then he flew at us, his legs splayed, his eyes wild.

I took off. I leaped off the garbage can and ran toward the hedges. Thunder crashed all around me, lightning lit up Mrs. Blackert's backyard, and rain poured from the sky, but I didn't care. I just wanted to get out of there. I scrambled under the hedges. I could hear Cara scuffling behind me and sweet little Felix hissing behind her.

What Do You Make of It?

As soon as we entered my room, I closed the door and pulled down the shade. It felt good to be enclosed within these familiar yellow walls. I ran my hand along my flowered comforter until it came to rest on the soft, rounded foot of Bongo Bear, a stuffed animal I've had since birth.

Cara was sitting cross-legged on my blue-and-yellow rug, pulling the rubber sole off her sneaker. There were little green needles from the hedge in her hair, her face was pale and streaked with dirt and rain.

"Well?" Cara asked me. Though I could tell that she was trying very hard to hide it, I heard a little quiver in her voice.

"That was weird." I sighed.

"Laura, that was more than weird!" she cried, forgetting all about her mangled sneaker. "That proves that Mrs. Blackert is a nasty old witch!"

I shook my head. "It proves she's crazy. It doesn't prove she's a witch." I should tell you that I'm a skeptic by nature. I need time to digest things. I needed time to think about all the wild things I'd seen in Mrs. Blackert's dining room. I wanted to make sure that my lively imagination hadn't gotten the best of me.

Cara, on the other hand, made up her mind quickly. "Come on, Laura," she said, wiping her streaky glasses on her T-shirt, "you saw that man in the painting make faces. You saw those cats dive into the picture. I hardly call that natural. I call that magic—black magic!"

I realized then that I hadn't imagined anything. Cara had seen the same peculiar things I had! There went my sensible theory about my overactive imagination. We couldn't have both imagined the same crazy things!

"What do you make of it, then?" I asked Cara.

"I've got a pretty good idea. But I want to think about it some more. I've got to get home now anyway." She looked at her watch.

Though she lived only one block away, Cara called

her father and asked him to pick her up. She said she had a stomachache, but I knew the truth. I knew that she was scared to walk home alone.

That night I couldn't sleep a wink. I stared at my window, waiting for Mrs. Blackert to crawl through it. Several times I thought I heard the window squeak open, and I pulled the sheets to my chin, watching Mrs. Blackert's powdery hands hanging over the sill, pulling her into my room. I saw her standing over my bed, her long white hair shimmering, smiling that crazy smile at me.

But of course when I blinked, it was only the moonlight, slipping past the shade.

The Tennis Tournament

I'd just drifted off to sleep when my mother knocked on my door. My mother was my alarm clock. Every morning she awakened me by calling out the same annoying thing, "Rise and shine!" in this high, cheerful voice. It was nice of her to wake me, but quite truthfully, that cheerful voice was hard to take in the morning. I rise because I have to, but it takes me a while to shine.

That morning I was shining less than ever.

When I peered into the mirror, I saw that I looked more like a raccoon than a twelve-year-old girl. My face was pinched and pointy, and there were black stains under my eyes.

"You look terrible," my mother remarked when I sat down for breakfast. "Are you sick?"

"I didn't sleep well," I mumbled.

"It's those ghost stories," my mother said sternly. "I don't approve of them. They upset you."

She herself looked very fresh and polished. She smelled nice, her hair was swept up in a yellow funnel, and her makeup was perfect. My mother always dressed nicely, even on weekends. She said she never knew when she'd be asked to show a house.

"Eat something." She pushed a bowl of cereal my way. "You're going to need your strength if you're going to beat Mary Jane!"

I ate some cereal, but I didn't beat Mary Jane. Tennis is like golf. To do well you have to concentrate, but I couldn't concentrate at all. Mrs. Blackert, the portrait, and the orange cats kept leaping and twirling before my eyes. I couldn't see the tennis ball. I swatted blindly at phantoms and spooks.

Mary Jane Benzer took home the trophy. It was so big that her mother had to carry it.

Later, when we were in the car driving home, Cara, who'd watched the tournament with my mother, said, "You really stank out there, Laura. But you were funny, running around in that silly white skirt, waving your racket about like you were swatting flies!"

I felt my face redden. I was mad. Believe it or not, I'd really wanted to win.

"But don't feel too bad, Laura. That girl Mary Jane is such a dog. She looks exactly like a boy!"

I couldn't help smiling. My mother, who overheard, said, "It's her hair. A woman should never chop her hair like that. Hair is a woman's crown jewel."

Cara poked me and snorted into my ear.

The Man in the Portrait

That evening I was just finishing dinner when Cara showed up at the kitchen door with Nimbo. She pressed her nose against the screen, and Nimbo did too. I guess they both smelled fried chicken.

"It's creepy Cara," Lucy muttered under her breath.

"Can I be excused?" I asked, shooting Lucy a dirty look.

"You may," my father said. He was loading the dishes into the dishwasher. We took turns.

I wrapped a chicken leg in a napkin for Cara. I knew she'd probably had some awful bean concoction for dinner and was probably dying of hunger.

I was filling two glasses with lemonade when my mother whispered in my ear, "Just make sure *that dog* doesn't relieve himself on my flowers. It kills them. Wilts them right down to the ground!" Like I said, she was crazy about those plants. I nodded.

I stepped outside and handed Cara the chicken leg.

"You're the best!" she cried, stuffing the leg into her mouth. In three bites it was gone.

Cara, Nimbo, and I went into my backyard. The moon was still almost full, and so bright I could see my shadow on the lawn. Cara and I plopped down at the patio table, facing each other. Nimbo slumped near Cara's feet. She poured some lemonade into her cupped palm, then reached down and gave him a little. Noisily, he lapped it up. I lit the citronella candle. Cara considered the wavy flame for a moment; then her eyes rose and slipped past my shoulder. I followed her gaze to Mrs. Blackert's house. It loomed in the shadows like a big, black, slumbering monster.

"I didn't sleep at all last night," Cara said, breaking the silence.

"I guess you could tell that I didn't either. I mean, I couldn't hit that tennis ball to save my life!" I replied, yawning.

"Last night, Laura, I sat up for hours, trying to make sense out of what we saw in that old witch's dining room. I guess I finally drifted off to sleep, because the next thing I knew, Nimbo was growling. When I opened my eyes, I saw that he was crouched on the floor near my bed. His teeth were bared and he was staring at the window.

"That cat, that little monster Felix, was on my

windowsill, Laura! I saw his silhouette! Nimbo went after him, but he ran away. Terrible, huh?"

"Awful," I agreed. I glanced uneasily at Mrs. Blackert's house.

We were silent for a while. Then Cara said, "After your great defeat in tennis I went to the library. I made a copy of an old newspaper picture of Doug Hirst the Third, Mrs. Blackert's missing husband. Here, take a look." Cara took a piece of paper out of her jean shorts, unfolded it, and pushed it toward me.

It was pretty dark on that patio, and the picture was a bit faded in some places and blotchy in others, but still I was able to make out the twisted nose and beady little eyes. This picture of Doug Hirst III looked like a younger, better-looking version of the repulsive man whose portrait hung on Mrs. Blackert's wall.

"Do you see the resemblance?" Cara asked eagerly.

I nodded slowly. I did. It was impossible not to.

"What are you getting at?" I asked hesitantly, not really wanting to hear the answer.

"I'm trying to say that the portrait in Mrs. Blackert's dining room *is* Doug Hirst the Third."

"How can that be?" I gasped, my head whirling. "Cara, according to that article you made me read, Mrs. Blackert painted a portrait of her husband years ago, when he was a young man. That ugly guy in the portrait was old, ancient. He was full of wrinkles. Maybe he's

Doug Hirst the First or Second. Doug Hirst the Third disappeared before he had a chance to grow old. So there's no way Mrs. Blackert could've painted him as an old man!" I was satisfied with my argument. To me it sounded very logical.

"What if he grew old *in the painting?*" Cara asked, her eyes wide and excited.

I looked at her, stunned. I never would've thought of that. It was outlandish, far-fetched, and altogether crazy! If it just happened to be true, I wanted no part of this entire affair!

"Laura," Cara drawled with exaggerated patience, "didn't you hear Mrs. Blackert call herself the portrait's wife?"

I shrugged. I had, but I couldn't bring myself to admit it.

"Even if you missed that," Cara continued, "you have to remember her saying that yesterday was the man in the portrait's hundredth birthday!" She looked at me expectantly.

I nodded. There was no way I could lie about that. Who could've missed that crazy caviar celebration?

"Well, I checked. Yesterday was Doug Hirst the Third's birthday. Yesterday Doug Hirst the Third would have been one hundred years old."

I groaned.

"You know what we have to do, don't you?" Cara

asked, her face as radiant as the citronella flame, her hands gripping the table's edge.

"We can forget about Mrs. Blackert for starters," I replied, though I knew this wasn't what she had in mind.

"No, Laura. We have to go see Doug Hirst the Third's business partner, Brad Deever, and ask him what went on all those years ago."

"Who? What?" I practically shrieked. "Deever? Why he's . . . he's probably—" I was going to say *dead,* but Cara cut me off.

"He's not dead, Laura. He's old, but he's still kicking. I tracked him down. He's living in a nursing home nearby. I thought we should at least talk to someone who was close to Mrs. Blackert and Doug Hirst. Maybe, after talking to him, you'll be as convinced as I am about that old witch!" She grinned at me.

I couldn't believe what I was hearing. I was dumbstruck, shocked by this preposterous idea.

"I say we go see him tomorrow!" She added, "Visiting hours are from one to four."

I knew then that she'd been planning this visit all day. And I didn't like it. In my opinion Cara was going too far, much too far.

"Well, I'm not going," I declared.

"Fine. I am." With that she and Nimbo huffed into the night.

Parsonage House

But Sunday morning I changed my mind. I decided to go with Cara after all.

That's because, while I was breakfasting on my father's famous banana pancakes, my mother told me that Mrs. Benzer had invited both of us over for lunch. A whole afternoon listening to Mary Jane blabber about her tennis victory and soap operas—it was unbearable, unthinkable. Though I'd hardly touched my breakfast, I couldn't eat another bite. I stared at my plate, watching my pancakes stiffen and my syrup congeal. Then I had an idea.

"Sorry, Mom," I said. "I already have plans with Cara."

"Can't you change them? I mean, it's not like you never see her."

"No, Mom, I can't. I promised we'd go visit this old uncle of hers in a nursing home. Her father can't make it—he's got some sort of march."

My whole family looked at me then rather curiously, but no one said a word. I knew my mother felt guilty telling me not to go. It wasn't as if Cara had a million relatives to visit. Actually, though I didn't mention this, I don't think she had any.

I was already outside when Cara came rattling down my driveway on her rusty old bike.

"I came to see if you'd had a change of heart." Cara

braked by backpedaling. That's how old her bike was—the brakes weren't on the handlebars.

"I have," I replied, dragging my bike, which used to be Lucy's, out of the garage. It's a ten-speed—a little too big for me, but manageable.

I hopped on and pedaled into the sunny afternoon.

"Hey," she called after me, "you don't even know where you're going!"

The nursing home was only a ten-minute bike ride from my house. It sat nestled in a neighborhood of pine and birch trees, at the end of a long, lonely road. Because of the tall, lush foliage, only the thinnest rays of sunlight fell upon its cool brick façade.

I'd expected the nursing home to appear boxy and industrial, like a hospital, but instead it looked like someone's estate. If it hadn't been for the cement "Parsonage House" engraving above the double white doors, I never would've believed we'd come to the right place.

There wasn't any rack for our bikes, so we just pushed them in among the trees. I took my time walking up the wide granite steps. It felt uncomfortably conspicuous entering the building. That's the trouble with small, quiet places: Everything you do is noticed.

Cara was eager and excited. She bounded up the steps and yanked one of the heavy white doors. It opened into a red-carpeted hallway. At the end of the corridor, a woman sat behind a desk.

"You gals must be Cara and . . . " she called out in a shrill voice.

"I'm Cara. That's Laura," Cara said, pointing to me.

I guess it'd been a pretty dull day at Parsonage House, because the woman had been polishing her nails. She rose from the desk, flapping her pink-tipped hands around in the air.

"I'm Ms. Cabage," she announced.

She had small blue eyes, which leaned into each other rather queerly, and dyed-blond hair with dark, earth-colored roots.

"This is an awfully strange-looking nursing home," Cara remarked, her eyes roving the wallpapered walls, paintings, and mirrors. She was right. The place looked more like a quaint old hotel.

Ms. Cabage said, "It's not a nursing home, honey. A nursing home is for folks who can no longer take care of themselves. Folks here can care for themselves all right; they just can't care for a house. So they all live here, like one big happy family. Ya gotta have a lot of the green stuff to stay in this joint, honey, if ya know what I mean."

Cara whispered to me, "If she calls me honey one more time, I'll puke."

I tried not to laugh.

Ms. Cabage led us to an elevator. "Follow me," she said. "Mr. Deever is waiting upstairs, in the library. He's a real sweetie pie. You'll love him. And he's just dying to meet you. He's simply been beside himself since you called."

I realized then how much work Cara had actually put into this meeting. I'd come to escape a grueling afternoon with Mary Jane. But Cara was here on a mission. It was clear to me that for her, this Mrs. Blackert thing was no longer a game—it was real, dangerously real.

And that scared me.

Brad Deever

Ms. Cabage said, "Here are those lovely young damsels you were expecting, Mr. Deever." Boy, was she corny. Then she whirled around, leaving us alone in the library with this very old man.

At first Mr. Deever, his thin body crumpled into a large wingback chair, reminded me of a floppy old scarecrow. But I soon saw that he was dressed too nicely to be a scarecrow. It was hot and stuffy in that library, yet he wore a blue cardigan sweater, a yellow bow tie, a pair of gray flannel trousers, and shiny black dress shoes.

I wasn't positive, but I got the feeling that he'd gotten dressed up just for us. And that was touching, it really was. It made me like him.

Ms. Cabage had told us that Mr. Deever was ninety-eight, and that he was blind. But his face, despite a web of wrinkles, looked very lively and distinct. His big old nose kept twitching up and down, just like a rabbit's, and his ears, which were pretty enormous, flapped like wings. Oddly enough, he still had a full head of brown hair, and I wondered if Ms. Cabage, who looked awfully fond of bleach herself, dyed it for him.

The library was pretty nice. It was wood paneled and brimming with books. I was dying to inspect all the titles, but Cara started talking right away. She wanted to get right down to business.

"Like I said on the phone, Mr. Deever, Laura and I are trying to write an article for our school paper about the disappearance of your ex–business partner, Doug Hirst the Third, which happens to be the greatest unsolved mystery in Dove's Cove." You had to hand it to Cara, she was a pretty smooth liar.

"By golly, so it is," Mr. Deever agreed. He slapped his skinny thigh and said, "You've come to the right man, young ladies." His voice reminded me of a dirt road riddled with potholes—you could tell he'd gotten a lot of use out of it. "You see, I was Doug Hirst's business partner *and brother-in-law*."

"Really? You mean you were married to Doug Hirst's sister?" Cara asked, surprised.

Mr. Deever smiled sadly. He said, "Unfortunately, that's exactly what I mean. The papers never mentioned this. The Hirsts asked them not to. They didn't want Marcy's name getting dragged into her brother's muddy affairs.

"But yes"—he sighed heavily—"I married Marcy Hirst. She pulled the wool over my eyes. On the surface she was as enchanting as a princess, and it certainly didn't hurt that she was rich. But after we were married, I found out that she was a witch!"

"A witch! Her too!" Cara gasped, almost tumbling out of her chair. That was the thing about Cara—ever since she'd read that book, you couldn't just call someone a witch without her taking you seriously.

Mr. Deever chuckled. "I meant that figuratively, though forty years with Marcy definitely made me believe in witches."

Cara blurted, "I believe in witches too!"

I was afraid she was missing the point, so I said quickly, "Mr. Deever, please tell us more about Doug Hirst!"

Mr. Deever's elephantine ears gave a little wiggle. "Of course," he said agreeably. "Doug was just like his sister, Marcy. Rotten. Yes sirree. And I mean *rotten*. Picture an egg that's been in the refrigerator for a good ten years, and you'll know what I mean. Ha, ha, ha."

I sure knew what he meant about rotten eggs. I said, "Once in our fridge I found this egg—"

But Cara cut me off. She'd already heard about that

stinky old egg. "Mr. Deever, please go on," she said, frowning at me.

"Well, Marcy and Doug did have one thing going for them, by golly, and that was charm, a penetrating, poisonous charm. Like venom. Both Addy and I fell for that charm hook, line, and sinker."

"Addy?" Cara echoed.

"Why, yes," said Mr. Deever, "that's what Adele liked to be called. It was her nickname."

"I see," Cara replied thoughtfully.

I myself didn't see a thing. There were times, like now, when I just couldn't follow Cara's thoughts. I mean, what was the big deal about the name Addy?

I decided to ask something a little more basic. I said, "How'd Doug Hirst meet Mrs. Blackert in the first place?"

"Ah," Mr. Deever answered. "I remember that as though it were yesterday. He met her in Brigham, Massachusetts, at an exhibition of the Blackert portraits. I'd heard that they were spectacular, so I joined Doug. They were the most fascinating portraits I'd ever seen. Very realistic, almost unsettling.

"But Doug didn't even glance at the portraits. He had no appreciation for art whatsoever. 'Art is garbage,' he said."

"Why'd he go to an art show if he didn't like art?" Cara asked. I'd been wondering about that myself.

"Good question, good question," Mr. Deever responded, his nose hopping in the air. "He went because he'd heard about the Blackert sisters. Heard they were beauties. And by golly they were.

"But out of all the Blackert sisters, Addy was the prettiest. She was simply spellbinding with that unbelievable red hair, that dangerous hair. Doug flipped when he saw her. Followed her around like a puppy. The problem, young ladies, was that none of the Blackerts, Addy included, liked him."

"Why?" I asked.

"I don't know why exactly," Mr. Deever said. "But I can tell you what I think. I think they saw right through to Doug's shriveled little heart. The whole time he was in that gallery, they stared at him queerly, their dark eyes boring into him like drills.

"Doug, though, was not discouraged by that. He was what you call a lady-killer. To him Addy was a challenge. 'I'll get her, just you see,' he told me.

"He started going up to Massachusetts every weekend, just to visit Addy. He wined and dined her. Sent her flowers every day. One time he even took her sailing. Marcy and I went along too. The whole time we were out at sea, Doug was leaning over the rail, his face as green and puckered as a pickle.

" 'Sailing is the pits,' he griped. 'This boat is like a roller coaster, up and down, up and down. It's making me sick. Besides, who in his right mind wants to be out at sea with a bunch of big, smelly fish?'

"Certainly Addy did. I told my old friend Dougie boy to just look at her. If anyone was enjoying the sailing, it was she. Let me tell you, she had a smile on her face as big as the sea, especially when we saw some dolphins.

"Doug, his mind always plotting and conniving, said, 'This ought to get her to marry me.'

"The funny thing was, he was right. After that she did marry him. I guess she was touched by the fact that he had taken her sailing even though he knew he'd get seasick."

Mr. Deever paused for a second, then tipped a gnarly hand toward us and said, "Will any of this help you write your article?"

I was so engrossed in his story that I'd forgotten all about that stupid lie we'd told him. I almost said, "What article?" But at the last minute I caught myself.

Cara, who'd been scribbling like crazy into a homework pad, and who was, naturally, as sharp as ever, remarked, "Sure will!"

Mr. Deever looked pleased. He said, "They'd been married about three years when Doug disappeared."

"What do you think happened to him?" Cara asked.

Mr. Deever scratched his head pensively. "I think Doug probably ran off with some hot tamale from South America and got himself killed. That's what the police and FBI thought at first too, but later, when they couldn't find any trace of him—he hadn't booked himself on any boats and he hadn't withdrawn a cent from the bank—they gave up that theory."

"What'd they do then?" Cara pressed.

"They started sniffing around Adele—went after her like a pack of bloodhounds."

"Why?" I asked. I have to say that at that moment, I felt a little sorry for Mrs. Blackert. I pictured people swarming around her big gray house. I imagined them crashing through her hedges, plowing through her yard, and peering into her windows—doing, I realized guiltily, all the things Cara and I'd done.

"You know how it is," said Mr. Deever. "They always suspect the spouse."

"Did they find any evidence linking Mrs. Blackert to her husband's disappearance?" Cara asked, looking up from her pad.

"Not a single thing, young lady. Not that they didn't try! They dug up her garden, ransacked her house, all to no avail! And Addy, she just stuck to her preposterous story—that her husband was living in his portrait."

"What'd all those detectives say to *that*?" Cara asked.

"Well, eventually they made her take that portrait off the wall. Thought maybe she'd killed Doug and buried his body behind it. But that wall was solid as a rock, not a scratch mark on it."

I shot Cara a look. If Doug Hirst was actually in that portrait, like Cara said, then why was there nothing behind it? How could he exist in a flat canvas? It just didn't make sense.

Cara ignored me. "What happened next?" she asked.

"The police and FBI dropped the case. I guess they had to. As they say, without a body you can't have a murder. Besides, Doug Hirst the Third wasn't the only missing guy on the planet!"

"What about the Hirsts?" Cara exclaimed. "Didn't *they* do anything? I mean, Doug Hirst *was* their one and only son!"

"So he was, young lady, so he was. But don't think that meant anything to the Hirsts! No sirree. Doug could've moved to the moon for all they cared, so long as he kept the Hirst name out of the papers.

"You see, the Hirsts hated one another. Couldn't stand to be in each other's company. Each thought the other was miserable, when the truth was that *they were all miserable.*

"Anyway, Doug's parents didn't even know he was missing till they saw his name splattered across the headlines. You should've seen them then. They were crazed. Phoned Marcy up. Asked her if she'd heard about her brother. And you know what Marcy said?"

Cara and I both said we didn't.

"She said, 'Yeah, I heard. What of it?' Real blasé.

"So the Hirsts said, 'Why didn't you tell us? All this time has gone by and we haven't *done* anything. What'll the papers say about that?' You see, that was all they cared about—how they *seemed,* not how they actually *were*.

"Marcy said, 'Get off my back! I just forgot.'

"So the Hirsts hired a private investigator, an ex-cop, a grimy fellow by the name of Mete. They told him to check up on Addy, see if she was involved."

"Why'd they suspect her?" asked Cara. She sat forward in her chair, all bug-eyed and interested.

"They hated her even more than they hated each other. I think they wanted to make her life difficult."

"Why'd they hate her?" I asked. Poor Mrs. Black-ert—no one ever gave her a break.

"They never forgave her for not using the family name. Said she was arrogant."

"Wow," I said. They sounded arrogant to me.

Mr. Deever recalled, "That Inspector Mete was a big, dumb, lazy fellow. You could *give* the guy a clue, label it and everything, and by golly I think he still wouldn't know what to do with it! That's how dumb he was! Not surprisingly, he couldn't come up with any reasonable evidence linking Addy to Doug's disappearance. He just kept babbling about these portraits in her dining room, said there was something peculiar about them."

76

"What?" Cara shouted. "What was peculiar about them?" She clutched the arms of her chair.

"If you ask me, nothing was queer about them," barked Mr. Deever. "They were simply portraits, expertly painted. I'm sure that Mete fella just didn't know anything about art. Had probably never seen a portrait before in his life!"

"But what'd he *say* about the portraits?" Cara persisted.

"Nothing, because shortly after mentioning them, Mete disappeared—"

"What?" Cara gaped.

"What I said, young lady, was that Inspector Mete vanished. You see, he used to give the Hirsts an update on their son's case every Friday. Not that he ever had anything interesting to say. Then he'd collect his paycheck and leave. But one Friday Mete didn't show up. Never showed up again."

"What do you think happened to him?" Cara asked. She was leaning way over in her chair, staring at Mr. Deever. I saw a sharp glint in her eye.

Mr. Deever said, "No one knows."

"I bet I know," Cara muttered.

"What was that, young lady? Speak up. I'm a little hard of hearing!"

"I said is there anything else you can tell us?"

Mr. Deever said, "Well yes, there is. About a year after Doug disappeared, my wife, Marcy, told me that wherever Doug was, she hoped he'd stay put! This way, she said, the whole Hirst fortune would go to her!"

Now *that* was a nasty woman! As much as I'd joked about wishing Lucy would disappear, I didn't mean it. But this woman, Marcy, sounded serious!

Then Cara asked a very strange question.

"Mr. Deever, I'm curious. What did Inspector Mete look like?"

Mr. Deever considered this for a moment; then he said, "Can't see as it matters. But if you really want to know, he looked like a great big slab of baloney."

I wanted to laugh. I mean, what a crazy description! But Cara didn't look like she thought it was crazy at all. She was writing something down. I wasn't sure what it was, but it looked an awful lot like "baloney."

Believe it or not, Mr. Deever still wasn't finished with his story. He said, "That Addy was a pretty spectacular woman. To get away from that miserly wife of mine, I started visiting her. I felt sorry for her. She was so lonely, so harassed. No wonder she acted so odd. We sat in that big old house of hers, drinking tea and talking.

"One day she said, 'You know, Brad, after we were married, Doug told me how much he'd hated sailing and those dolphins we saw, that he hated all animals. He said he even hated me. He was quite different from what I thought. He was an ogre, a fiend. I never should've married him. I should've listened to my sisters and mother.'

"She looked at me sadly. There were tears in her big black eyes.

"Then she said, 'Do you know what he did? He murdered my pet cat—drowned the poor fellow in a bucket of water, then stuffed him and stuck him over the mantel, as if he were a painting.' She started to cry.

"It was terrible, watching her shed all those tears. You see, her tears were black. Like oil. Like her eyes. Addy said that was because of her makeup."

I could barely digest a thing he was saying. As soon as I heard that bit about the cat, I started to feel nauseous.

Cara didn't seem bothered at all. She said, cool as a cucumber, "Hmmm. . . . I bet that Adele Blackert hated Doug Hirst. I bet she wanted him to disappear. Mr. Deever, don't you agree?"

Mr. Deever said, "Well, I'm sure, in a way, she did. There were quite a few times when I hoped Marcy would disappear too!"

Cara shot me a triumphant look.

I was still feeling ill. I glanced at Mr. Deever. I could tell he wanted to talk some more about Mrs. Blackert, that he *liked* talking about her.

But when, after a moment, he started talking again, his voice sounded different. It sounded faraway. "I had a lot of fun with Addy. Took her for drives, mostly to amusement parks. She loved the rides.

"'They're almost like magic,' she'd tell me. She said that every time I took her on a ride.

"We'd go out to eat once in a while," Mr. Deever recalled. His voice sounded so dreamy, I wasn't even sure if he remembered we were in the room. "Just me and Addy. We ate tacos. Addy loved them. 'You cannot get a good taco back in England, Brad,' she'd say."

He sighed. "Marcy didn't like me going around with Addy. But I didn't care. Addy made me happy, and Marcy, well, she was a miserable old witch.

"Then I started having trouble with my eyes." He pointed to those two vacant orbs. "Retinal degeneration, said the doctor. Marcy took me to some clinic in Switzerland to get them fixed, but as you can see, the operation wasn't successful.

"When we returned home, Marcy broke the news to me. She told me that while we were gone, Addy Blackert sold her house and moved back to England. Suddenly I didn't care about being blind," he said, his voice muddy, dark. "What was there to see?"

He shrank in his chair. It looked like the arms and the cushions were swallowing him.

I was stunned. What an awful story! How could Brad Deever's wife tell such a terrible lie? I wondered if we should tell him the truth—that Mrs. Blackert still lived in the house next door to me. But maybe it wasn't wise. Perhaps it'd be too great a shock for him.

Just then Ms. Cabage barged into the room carrying a little brass box and a glass of water.

"Time for you little ladies to go," she announced crisply. "Mr. Deever needs to take his pills!"

School

On Tuesday, when school started, I was glad. I hoped that school would distract Cara. Perhaps she'd be much more interested in the eighth grade than in Mrs. Blackert. All the years that Mrs. Blackert had lived next door to me, I'd left her alone and she'd left me alone. I liked it that way.

Surprisingly, I enjoyed my first day back at school. Eliza and Jan had gone to camp for the second half of the summer, and they had tons of stories, none of which had anything to do with witches.

But when the bus dropped me off, I saw Cara sitting on the curb outside my house. I knew, just looking at her, that she wasn't going to let me off the hook when it came to Mrs. Blackert.

"I forgot how ugly that was!" she cried, jumping to her feet when I got off the bus.

"I hadn't." We were referring to my uniform, which I always expected to see on a list of fashion "don'ts."

Cara and I didn't go to the same school. Cara went to

public school. She walked to school, and she wore whatever she wanted. I attended a private all-girls school. I had to take a bus and wear this hideous uniform: a white shirt, a green-plaid skirt, and brown socks. In that green-and-brown uniform, Cara said I looked like someone's sick idea of a tree, and she was right.

"So how's seventh grade?" Cara asked me, smiling.

"Okay," I replied. "They built this new library over the summer. It has a fake fireplace. They had it on today, even though it's burning hot outside."

I should tell you what happened to our old school library, because it was sort of a big deal. I mean, it was in the newspaper, and for a while it was all anyone talked about. Last year this crazy girl in my grade burned the library down with her mother's cigarette lighter. One day she was alone in the library helping the librarian, Mrs. Snupf. When Mrs. Snupf left the room for a moment, the girl took out the lighter and set fire to a book, and the fire traveled to another book, and so on. I bet she was trying to burn the whole entire school down, but Mrs. Snupf returned just in time. The minute she got a whiff of the smoke, she pulled the alarm.

I'd been through a million phony fire drills in which we marched, single file, out and then back into the school. No big deal. But this was different. This was the real thing. Thick gray smoke rolled like storm clouds down the halls. I got the uncomfortable feeling it was chasing us. A couple of girls started to scream. Though I managed to hold myself together pretty well, I was glad to see the bright-red fire trucks parked outside. There were so many of them on the street, it looked like a parade.

For a long time I stood with Eliza and Jan, shivering in the cold, damp air watching the firemen, in their big hats and yellow coats, squirt my school. Luckily, no one was hurt, if you don't count all those library books. And that's why they built a new library in my school—because the old one was nothing but ashes.

The girl who set the fire was named Beth, but only the teachers called her that. Everyone else called her Snake Eyes, because her eyes were the color of yellow reflectors, and they were split in the middle by long black slits, just like a snake's.

I guess Snake Eyes bragged about setting the fire, because someone told. She was expelled, and the school brought charges against her. But then something quite astonishing happened—Snake Eyes disappeared! She vanished without a trace. Her parents begged the police to find her, but their investigation didn't turn up anything. Beth Login was gone.

Witch Theories

"Well, in case you're wondering, the eighth grade is exactly like the seventh!" Cara declared.

"Great!" I replied sarcastically.

While I changed into normal clothes, Mrs. O set out homemade brownies and milk. Mrs. O's brownies were amazing—they were almost like fudge. I knew she'd made them as a special treat for our first day back at school.

Cara and I took our snacks outside to eat so that we could talk privately without Mrs. O overhearing our conversation. She pretended she was mashing potatoes, cleaning out the refrigerator, or mopping the floor, but I could see by the tilt of her head that she was really listening to us. I liked Mrs. O but sometimes I was sure that she was also a spy for my mother.

"Listen, Laura, I figured out a lot of stuff after our meeting with Mr. Deever," Cara proclaimed as she munched on her brownie.

Though two days had passed since our meeting with Mr. Deever, we had not yet discussed what he'd said. Following our visit to Parsonage House, Cara had bolted home. She'd promised her father that she'd go to the movies with him.

The next day, Labor Day, I didn't see Cara. Every year my family and the Benzers have the same dreary little picnic in the park. While everyone else played games, Mary Jane filled me in on her favorite soaps. They all sounded exactly the same. I wondered how she kept them straight.

You might think I was dying to talk about what Mr. Deever had told us, but quite honestly I wasn't. As I mentioned, I wanted to forget about Mrs. Blackert. So instead of encouraging Cara, I merely stared at the chewy brownie on my plate.

"Don't you want to know what I figured out?"

"I'm not sure," I replied truthfully. But often Cara heard only what she wanted to hear. This being the case, she took my response as a yes.

"First of all," she said, "I think that Deever proved, beyond a shadow of a doubt, that Mrs. Blackert is a witch!"

He had? I stared at Cara doubtfully.

"Look Laura, he dropped about a zillion clues. He said Mrs. Blackert was 'spellbinding' and that her hair was 'dangerous.' He claimed she cried black tears, and he said she kept babbling about amusement park rides and how they're like magic. He even told us how Mrs. Blackert wanted to be called Addy, as in adder, Laura. What a perfect witch name!"

"Adder?" I repeated blankly.

Cara frowned. "An adder," she said in her best know-it-all voice, "is a European snake. Addy, short for adder, is such a suitably evil name for a British witch! It's too much of a coincidence to ignore. Besides," she added, "Mr. Deever said he *believed* in witches. I bet he knew that Mrs. Blackert was a witch, but he was probably too embarrassed to tell us!"

Clearly, Cara had stretched and twisted things beyond recognition. Listening to her, I wasn't even sure we'd both been at the same meeting!

She went on, unaware of my confusion, "Now I'm absolutely certain that that wicked old witch put a spell on her husband. She imprisoned him in that painting. Even Mr. Deever said he believed Mrs. Blackert *wanted* her husband to disappear. Didn't you hear him say that? Huh?"

I shrugged. I had, but I wasn't sure he'd meant it literally, the way Cara did.

"I bet that's what happened to the inspector too, that Mete guy. I bet his portrait is hanging in Mrs. Blackert's dining room right now. Along with that reporter, Carl Hilb. No wonder old Mrs. Hilb was so spooked by the portrait of her son," Cara cried. She sounded very proud of herself.

"So?" I asked cautiously. I was thinking, Live and let live. Even if she was right, even if Mrs. Blackert did indeed stick people in paintings, fine! I didn't want any part of it. I didn't want her sticking *me* in a painting!

"What do you mean, *so?* That's big, Laura! It means Mrs. Blackert is a real witch!"

"If she's a real witch, Cara," I said slowly, "I don't want anything to do with her!" Never had I spoken truer words!

"You mean you can just forget about all those poor people she imprisoned in those paintings? You mean you can just leave them there, in those canvases, to rot?" Cara looked incredulous.

"Yup."

"Well, I can't, Laura! I'm going to think of a way to rescue them!"

"But what if they're evil?" I ventured.

This was the question that'd been bothering me all along. I recalled that portrait of Doug Hirst III. I saw it so clearly, it was almost as though it were hanging in my mind. In my opinion, if anyone was evil, it was he. Hadn't Mr. Deever said that Doug Hirst III was rotten? Hadn't he echoed what Mrs. Blackert herself had said in her dining room—about Hirst having drowned her poor cat? Maybe Carl Hilb had ended up in a painting for a good reason too. A barnacle, Cara had called him. A barnacle didn't sound like a nice creature. And Inspector Mete hadn't sounded all that terrific either—grimy and lazy, Mr. Deever had called him. Maybe Mrs. Blackert had had good reasons for what she'd done!

I mentioned this to Cara, but she wouldn't be persuaded.

"Those portraits aren't evil, Laura. They're victims of Mrs. Blackert's wickedness!"

"I don't know, Cara," I replied. "Mr. Deever's wife,

Marcy, sounded much worse than Mrs. Blackert." I shuddered, remembering how she'd lied to her husband, telling him that Mrs. Blackert had moved back to England.

"You're wrong. Marcy was selfish and greedy. Mrs. Blackert is evil. There's a difference."

Was there? I wasn't sure.

But there was no point arguing any further. As I've said, you couldn't reason with Cara when she had an idea lodged in her head. Sometimes you just had to let her be.

Burglars

One chilly Saturday in September Cara came over to my house looking very peculiar. She was dressed entirely in black. She wore a black turtleneck, black jeans, and shiny black dress shoes, which looked terrible with her jeans. She'd stuffed her hair into a black baseball cap. A few limp strands dangled about her face.

"Let me guess," Lucy said. "You're going to be a burglar for Halloween?"

Cara smirked at her. They didn't really get along. Cara claimed that my sister was ditzy, and Lucy said that Cara was a goon.

Cara and I went up to my room.

"Why *are* you dressed like that?" I asked.

"For once," Cara said, "Lucy wasn't entirely wrong."

"You mean *that's* what you're going to wear for Halloween?" I was hurt. I couldn't believe she'd planned her costume without me. Cara and I'd always planned our Halloween costumes together.

The previous Halloween we'd dressed as a two-headed monster. We took a bedsheet and lined it with crumpled newspaper, so that it was fat at one end and skinny at the other. Then we rolled the stuffed sheet and stapled the folds. Finally, we painted the stuffed sheet green, then pinned the fat end to the rear of my uncle Arthur's pants. Uncle Arthur is fat enough for Cara and me each to stand comfortably in one leg of his pants. We wore crazy wigs on our heads, covered our skin with fake scars and vampire blood, and put plastic fangs in our mouths. It was such a good getup that we won Most Original Costume in the town contest. But it was hard to walk in those pants. We had to waddle and hop. Needless to say, we didn't get a whole lot of trick or treating done.

This year we were trying to think up something extra good. We figured it'd be our last year dressing up, being that we were almost teenagers.

"No, I'm not going to dress like this for Halloween," Cara said, dramatically. "But I am trying to look like a burglar."

Inwardly I moaned. Cara had that gleam in her eyes, which told me that she was up to something.

"What black clothes do *you* have, Laura?"

"Why?" I asked, suspicious.

"Because we're going to sneak into Mrs. Blackert's house and rescue that man in the painting. Then we'll find out the truth about Mrs. Blackert. She's away, you know," Cara said slyly. "The postman told me."

"What do you mean, the postman told you?" Since when did Cara have conversations with the postman?

"He told me one day last week, when he delivered the mail."

"Why?" It wasn't very reassuring to hear that the postman ran around telling everyone who was home and who wasn't!

Cara groaned. Sometimes she got impatient with my questions. She said, "I asked him what Mrs. Blackert was like. I figured maybe he'd know, since he's there every day, delivering her mail. He didn't know, but he said that it was funny I asked, because he'd just spoken to her. Mrs. Blackert asked him to hold her mail while she was away. She's gone, Laura. The house is empty!"

Not really, I thought, picturing those awful portraits.

"Look," I said in my most rational voice, "we can't just break into her house. It's illegal. If we get caught, we'll be put in jail. It'll go on our records. Besides, Cara, it's daylight. Why do we have to wear black?"

"First of all, Laura, burglars *always* wear black," Cara said irritably. "Secondly, the whole idea is not to get

caught. And for your information, imprisoning innocent people in paintings is probably illegal too.

"Come on, Laura," she coaxed, "haven't I been a
good best friend? Didn't I get those stupid boys off
your back? When was the last time any of them stuck
gum in your hair? Huh? You mean to tell me that after
all I've done for you, you won't do this one little thing
for me?"

As I've said, Cara had a way with words.

Breaking In

Before I knew it, I was putting on what Cara called burglar clothes. I shoved my yellow hair into a black beret,
threw on a black sweatshirt, and climbed into black leggings and black sneakers. I even put on a pair of black
gloves, so that no one would be able to trace my finger-
prints. I peered at myself in the mirror. I looked like a
skinny little thief.

Outside, it was very gray and dreary, as though a dark
cloud had descended over the whole neighborhood.
The street was deserted, and a chill had crept into the
air. It was a spooky day, a day when it's easy to believe in
ghouls and ghosts and witches.

Since I wasn't very keen about crawling through the
hedges to get to Mrs. Blackert's house, I suggested that
we take a more direct route and sneak up Mrs. Blackert's front walk.

"What if someone drives by and sees us, two black-clad figures creeping up a walkway?" she said, frowning. "You know how nosy everyone is around here! They'll call the police!"

I nodded glumly.

Mrs. Blackert's backyard looked worse than I remembered. Most of her flowers were dead. Those that weren't were too wilted and droopy to lift their heads. The leaves on her bushes and trees were so brown, they looked black.

"I know how we'll get inside the house," Cara whispered to me.

"Great," I mumbled.

Cara pointed to Mrs. Blackert's old greenhouse. In the gray daylight I could see that it was in terrible shape. Its roof was made of crisscrossing strips of wood. The crisscrosses formed squares that should've been filled with glass, but most of it was missing. The glass that was there looked as though it might cave in at any minute.

"All this week," Cara confided, "I've been snooping around, trying to find a way into that freaky house. Finally, I peeked through those French doors"—she pointed to a pair of glass doors that sat atop a stoop and opened into the backyard—"and saw a door to the greenhouse that's partly open. It leads into the house."

I was a bit surprised. Until then Cara hadn't told me

that she'd spent the week prowling around Mrs. Black-ert's backyard. I was shocked at her secrecy—usually we told each other everything. Then it dawned on me that Cara hadn't told me because she knew I wouldn't approve. I didn't. To me, prowling around Mrs. Black-ert's house seemed dangerous. I remembered that re-porter, Carl Hilb the barnacle, and what had happened to him when he'd spied on the Blackerts. And what about Inspector Mete?

"You'll climb through there, Laura," Cara said, point-ing to the top of the greenhouse, " 'cause you're smaller than me. Then you can unlock the French doors."

I gulped. What, I wondered, had I gotten myself into?

Cara gave me a boost. I climbed onto the green-house, my hands gripping the wobbly wooden frame. Then I lowered myself through one of the glassless squares. I landed on a dirty shelf that had probably been meant to hold plants. The greenhouse was really a mess. Clay pots, watering cans, and rusty gardening tools lay everywhere, and I was certain that every variety of weed was growing up from the floor. I hoped there was no poison ivy. I had it once and I itched for a week.

At the far end of the greenhouse I saw a door. Just as Cara had said, it was open a crack. I jumped off the shelf and crept quietly to the door. I pressed my ear to it. I held my breath and listened, but all I could hear was the thudding of my heart. I pushed the door open very slowly.

There was a horrible cry, a high, shrill scream. Then, out of the blackness, something flew at my face, screeching. I choked, unable to cry out. Little gurgling noises escaped from my throat. I waited for claws to rip into my skin, so certain was I that one of Mrs. Blackert's orange cats was attacking me for trespassing. But then the thing swooped upward, and I knew that it was a bat. Probably it'd been sleeping in the dark hallway beyond the greenhouse. I must have scared it as much as it had scared me.

I sighed and sank to the floor. My knees were weak. I was sure that my heart was setting an all-time speed record.

I was in a dark hall. The brick floor was so cold, I could feel its icy surface through my leggings. The walls were covered with moldy green wallpaper. I jumped. I heard something—a tapping. But it was only Cara, standing outside on the stoop, knocking softly on the French doors. I unlocked the doors and let her in.

"What happened?" she asked me when she was inside. "I heard a funny noise."

"A bat," I said. "From now on *you* go first."

Ahead of us stood a door. We both stared at it. It looked heavy and forbidding.

"Get Me Out of Here!"

The door led into Mrs. Blackert's kitchen, which was large, dark, and old-fashioned. It was clean—there were no dishes in the sink or crumbs on the counter—but it had an unused, forgotten look. A big black stove stood in one corner, the kind you see in black-and-white movies, and there was a long wooden table pressed against a wall. There was nothing on the table or on the stove, not a pot, a fork, or a glass.

Cara tiptoed through the kitchen. I followed close behind. Our feet made little shuffling noises on the floor.

She pushed open another door.

We were in Mrs. Blackert's dining room.

It was dim in the room. Only a few weak rays of light had managed to squeeze their way between the heavy drapes that framed the windows. Still, I could see, directly in front of me, the gruesome portrait of Doug Hirst III. He was gazing at us, and there was a strange glint in his eyes. I had the uncomfortable feeling that he was happy to see us, though I was not happy to see him. I looked around quickly and gasped. Eyes slid, dipped, rose—and some stared straight ahead—resting with a glittering eagerness on Cara and me. The portraits were watching us!

I grabbed Cara's arm. "Let's get out of here," I pleaded.

"Wait, Laura. I have to know if that's really Doug Hirst the Third," she hissed in my ear. She shook my hand off her arm and turned to the portrait.

"Tell me," she asked the painting in a loud, quivering voice, "are you Doug Hirst the Third?"

I held my breath, both awed by Cara's courage and filled with dread. The room was very silent. It felt the way the air does sometimes before a big rainstorm, saturated, dangerous, and heavy. Before me a cloud of dust motes swirled in a sliver of gray light. I was overcome with the desire to be one of those dust motes, because they looked so indistinguishable, so ungraspable, so completely safe.

Then a word sliced through the silent room.

"Y-e-sss. . . ."

I told myself that the portrait couldn't have spoken. I told myself that it was only steam I heard—the warm, moist breath of steam escaping from a radiator. But I knew I was only kidding myself, because the sound was too evil and menacing.

I forced myself to scrutinize the portrait. I had to. The face had changed. The watery blue eyes bulged. The lips were spread thinly across the face; covering them were flecks of white spit.

I was horrified. There was no question that the face

was different. It was a thousand times more dreadful than before!

I wanted to run, but my feet felt like cement blocks. I couldn't move. I could only stare helplessly at that awful portrait.

Then the man in the painting said, very distinctly, "Get me out of here!"

He was looking at Cara.

"Huh?" She could barely speak.

"I said *get me out of here!*"

Cara was staring, transfixed, at the portrait, her mouth open slightly, her glasses near the blunt tip of her nose. She didn't bother to push them up.

"Come a little closer," coaxed the portrait. The voice was oily, imploring.

I opened my mouth. I wanted to tell Cara that we should turn around and run, get out of there as fast as we could. I wanted to tell her that we shouldn't be rescuing this terrible monster, but the words spun around in my head; I couldn't hang on to them long enough to get them out of my mouth.

"I can see that you're a good little girl, a smart girl," Doug Hirst III said to Cara. "I'm sure you know that the woman who owns this house is a wicked witch! Listen to me, little girl. That woman shut me away in this loathsome painting because I know the truth about her! I've been in here so many years, I stopped counting. I've missed the best years of my life, and I need you to help me get out!"

His voice rose. It was trembly and shrill. It seemed to me that he was getting a little hysterical.

"And she lets those cats in here. Those filthy, flea-ridden beasts. She knows I hate them, despise their prickly whiskers, their sharp, pointed teeth, their putrid odor. She lets them in here just to torture me!"

I shuddered. All of the man's face was twisted now, not just his nose. He was truly a revolting sight. Surely, I thought, Cara could see this!

"All I need you to do, little girl, is lift this canvas off the wall and carry me out of this cursed house, away from that evil woman. Do it now—take me before she comes back with those cats!"

I didn't think Cara would do it. I was sure she'd be her bold, tough self and do what I wanted desperately to do but didn't have the guts to—laugh at that terrible portrait. I was certain that she had given up the idea of rescuing Doug Hirst III, that she saw how evil he was. But I was wrong. Cara took several steps toward the portrait. As she did, frothy white saliva dripped from his lips and slipped to the floor. Cara walked through the small pool of drool. She went up to the portrait. She put her hands on the frame.

With great effort I got the words out of me. "Cara," I

squeaked, "what are you doing? Come on, let's get out of here!"

"Shut up, you pathetic little twerp!" bellowed the man in the portrait, his eyes glaring at me.

His words stunned me into silence.

Cara stared at me blankly as if I were a complete stranger, not her very best friend. Her eyes were vacant, empty. I wondered if she was hypnotized.

She took the painting off the wall.

"Good," whispered the dreadful portrait of Doug Hirst III. I could hear him breathing; he was panting like a dog. "Hurry, hurry," he urged.

A Chorus of Portraits

"Take me too, you ugly maggot!"

I whirled around. I saw which portrait had spoken. It was that of a girl. She had a head of tight black curls and a pair of mean, yellow eyes—snake eyes, to be precise.

I knew her.

I don't know why I hadn't noticed her before. Perhaps I'd been too busy focusing on the portrait of Doug Hirst III. It was Beth Login—or Snake Eyes, as we called her— the girl who had set the school library on fire! What was *she* doing on Mrs. Blackert's dining-room wall?

Beth's snake-like gaze shifted from Cara to me. I saw a flicker of recognition ignite her face. I saw something small and pink dart out of her mouth. It was her tongue! Beth had stuck her tongue out at me!

I was dizzy. But before I could faint, the whole room exploded in sound.

"What about me, four eyes?"

"Don't forget me, cabbage breath!"

"Take me, you worthless slug!"

The portraits were all screaming at Cara. That dining room sounded louder than the bird house in the zoo. I spun around. A cold chill ran through me when I looked into the screeching, detestable faces. I didn't know how Mrs. Blackert, witch or no witch, could stand having them on her dining-room wall!

My eyes fell upon a painted face that looked exactly like a big, meaty slab of baloney. "In-inspector Mete!" I sputtered involuntarily.

The man grinned at me with his blubbery lips.

"Don't listen to them!" cried Doug Hirst III. "They're imbeciles. I'm the one who matters! Take me and run!"

But before Cara could do anything, the dining-room door swung open.

The Unexpected Happens

I heard all the portraits gasp. All, that is, except for Doug Hirst III.

"Run, you fool!" he barked at Cara. He looked desperate, wild. "Get me out of here!"

But Cara didn't move, and I didn't either. We stared helplessly at Mrs. Blackert, who was standing in the doorway.

For several agonizing minutes Mrs. Blackert stood perfectly still. She was wearing a long black cape; her white hair sprawled about her like a thick cobweb. One of her hands was clutching a broom, the other clasped a big, black portfolio, the kind painters use to carry their artwork. I watched the black circle of her eyes slowly travel about the room. For one long, torturous second they rested on me. I held my breath. I didn't swallow. I let a big gob of spit form in my mouth.

I was certain that I was about to choke when all at once, to my great relief, Mrs. Blackert's gaze shifted to Cara, who stood frozen, clutching the portrait of Doug Hirst III. A sudden movement beneath Mrs. Blackert's cape caught my eye. The orange cats crawled out of the cape, creeping stealthily toward Cara.

That's all I saw.

I screamed loudly, "Cara, run!" Then I turned around and took my own advice—I ran as fast as I could.

I heard a crash behind me, followed by a moan; then Doug Hirst's low, whining voice cried, "You little creep, you bumbling idiot, you . . ."

I didn't hear any more. I ran through the kitchen and into the dark hallway and out the French doors. I charged through the bushes and weeds and tore my way through the hedges. I didn't stop until I was in my backyard.

I almost collapsed with happiness when I saw my mother. She was planting tulip bulbs. I was delighted to see her doing such an ordinary, normal thing. I thought that perhaps, if I watched her for a few minutes, everything that had just happened would fade away like a bad dream.

But I didn't have a chance to watch her for very long. She whirled around when she heard me gasping for breath, and dropped her bulb planter.

"Laura! What happened to you?"

"Nothing, Mom. I was . . . I was . . . out playing a game!"

Without another word I dashed into the house. I knew if I stood there a second longer, my mother would interrogate me. She was really good at that. She never should've become a real estate agent. It was a waste of her talents. What she should've done was join the FBI.

I ran into my room. I was shaking all over. What, I wondered, had happened to Cara?

I looked out my window and breathed a sigh of relief. Cara was in my backyard, speaking with my mother. She looked terrible. Her clothes were torn and her hair was a mess. She'd lost the baseball cap. Her hands fluttered about her face as though she were crying. Cara never cried, not even during the saddest movies. I didn't think

Cara's eyes even had tear ducts! Then I realized that she wasn't crying. She had lost her glasses.

All at once a couple of orange cats came scampering onto the lawn. They started to surround Cara, but my mother shooed them away. She put her hand on Cara's shoulder, and the two of them walked toward the house. A couple of minutes later I heard their footsteps outside my room.

An Argument

"I don't know what kind of game you two were playing, Laura, but I don't like it," my mother said to me sternly as she led Cara into my room. "I need to finish planting before it rains, but you and I will talk later." She closed the door.

Cara turned to me. She squinted, struggling to see me. She looked very different. I couldn't believe how small her eyes were! Without those great slabs of glass in front of them, they no longer dominated her face. All by themselves her eyes looked kind of pale and puny. To me, at that moment, Cara no longer appeared tough. She looked harmless and sad, like a mole that can't find its way back into the earth.

"I can't believe you just left me there!" she said accusingly.

"Cara, I didn't know what to do! You were so weird! In the dining room, when I told you we should get out

103

of there, you just looked at me with this blank expression on your face. It was as if you didn't know me!"

Cara rubbed her eyes. I wondered how on Earth she was going to get through the day without her glasses.

"Laura, I was just trying to help that poor man! He's probably been stuck in that painting for a good fifty years! Anyway, do you know what I did before I ran out of there? I called Mrs. Blackert a witch. I did. I shouted, 'Witch,' and then I ran. I'm glad I did it too!"

"Cara," I said very slowly, trying to make my words sound important, "I don't think those portraits should be taken from that house. They're evil! I saw Beth Login, the girl who burned down my school library, hanging on Mrs. Blackert's wall, and she was a real creep!"

Cara stared at me like I was from another planet. For a moment I wondered if she'd even heard what I'd said. But she remarked, "Laura, Mrs. Blackert is the one who's evil. She's the creep! Maybe you're one also!"

Then she stormed out of my room, slamming the door behind her. I was mad, and I was shaken up. It was a lot to handle—seeing those horrible paintings in your neighbor's house, then having a big fight with your best friend.

While I sulked in my room, I did some serious thinking. I questioned why Cara couldn't see that those paintings were dangerous when, to me, it was as clear as day. Maybe her stubborn old mind was blocked. Maybe she was convinced Mrs. Blackert was an evil witch. But why evil? Hadn't Cara told me there were good witches and bad witches? How did we know Mrs. Blackert was bad? The only thing I knew for sure was that even if she was bad, those portraits were far worse.

I also knew that Cara had made a big mistake when she'd called Mrs. Blackert a witch. I bet Mrs. Blackert hadn't liked that too much. Now that she had Cara's glasses and her black baseball cap, there was no telling what she might do!

New Glasses

For about a week Cara and I avoided each other. During those days either I went home with Jan or Eliza, or else I played tennis. I tried to forget about that dreadful day in Mrs. Blackert's house. When something really bothers me, I pretend that a big vacuum cleaner has been let loose in my mind to suck up my troublesome thoughts. Sometimes this tactic works; sometimes it doesn't.

Meanwhile, I missed Cara. Jan and Eliza were nice, but they just didn't have her zing. I missed Cara's ghost stories. I missed telling her about school. I missed hearing her make fun of Mrs. O's hair.

But then one day Mrs. O showed Cara into the den, where I was reading.

"Hi!" Cara said. Her voice was very upbeat. I could tell that she wasn't angry anymore.

She looked different. At first I wasn't sure why, but then I noticed she was wearing new, funky glasses. They had thick black rims that swept upward at the outer edges, like gigantic cat eyes, but I didn't say that. I didn't want to bring up the subject of cats.

Instead I said, "Hey, I like your new glasses!"

"Pretty cool, huh?"

I nodded. Behind the glasses her eyes looked big again.

"I wanted to tell you that I thought up a great idea for our Halloween costumes," Cara said. She smiled broadly. I could tell she was very proud of those new glasses.

"Oh yeah?" I replied with interest. To tell you the truth, I'd kind of given up thinking about Halloween altogether. Though both Jan and Eliza (and good old Mary Jane Benzer, for that matter) had asked me to go trick or treating with them, I'd said no. The thought of Halloween without Cara depressed me. I'd begun to question whether Cara and I would ever be friends again. We'd never had a fight that had lasted as long as this one. More than once I'd thought of apologizing, but it was hard to apologize when I didn't even know what our fight was about!

"We'll be witches!" Cara exclaimed.

I almost fell off my chair. Was she kidding?

"But we'll give the witch thing a little twist. We'll be twin punk witches," she said triumphantly. "You can get glasses like mine. They've these tall hats too, real cool-looking, at Doogle's Drugstore downtown. They're made of fabric, not plastic. We'll wear short black skirts, crazy black stockings, and punk boots. Long black gloves too. Come on, Laura—it'll be fun. Unless you've got a better idea."

I didn't. Punk witches it was.

Halloween

On Halloween, instead of long black gloves, I wore my mother's red leather gloves, because Lucy said that was more of a punk thing to do. I wore Lucy's dark, slanted sunglasses, her black leather skirt (rolled up a couple of times at the waist), my black turtleneck, my black Lycra stockings, and her tall suede boots. I had to wear these heavy wool socks with the boots so they'd fit.

Cara dressed similarly, except that her skirt was not leather, her gloves were black, her boots were shorter, and of course she had her new cat glasses on. We both stuffed our hair into tall black witch hats. All in all, they weren't bad costumes.

Still, we didn't win Most Original Costume in the town contest. As luck would have it, Mary Jane Benzer won. Her costume wasn't even scary. She dressed up like an asparagus. How dumb! She had a hairy, dark-green asparagus tip on her head and a long, pale-green body. I didn't like the costume, but I guess if anyone was going to dress up like an asparagus, it made sense for it to be Mary Jane. She was tall and thin and narrow enough, and she did have a greenish complexion.

Cara was quiet while we trick-or-treated. I thought she was disappointed that we'd lost the contest. I was too, but I tried not to show it. Dressing up as punk witches had been Cara's idea, and I didn't want to insult her. It felt too good to be best friends again.

We trick-or-treated for a few hours. By dinnertime I was ready to call it quits. My candy bag was half full, and the sky was rapidly darkening. Soon it would be black. I also felt cold. There was an icy, wet sting in the air, which made me think that at any minute it might snow. The wind had picked up, whipping through every fiber of my cotton turtleneck. I wished I'd worn a jacket, but it would've ruined the effect of the costume.

We were almost at my house when Cara grabbed my arm.

"I've got an idea," she said.

"Oh no!" I groaned. I saw it, that dreaded mischievous gleam.

She ignored me. "Let's go trick or treating at Mrs. Blackert's house. It'll be a goof. She'll never recognize us in these outfits."

"Of course she will!" I cried, though neither Jan, Eliza, or Mary Jane Benzer, all of whom had been at the Halloween contest, had recognized me.

"Come on, Laura," Cara pleaded. "This is our last year of trick or treating. Don't you want to do something daring, something to end it with a bang? Something we'll look back on and laugh at?"

I sighed, wishing we'd won that stupid contest. The prize was a free dinner at Mr. Zarelo's pizza parlor. He had the best pizza in town. It was gooey with cheese, the way pizza should be. That would've been enough of a bang for me. But we hadn't won, and really, the day hadn't been very special.

I glanced at Mrs. Blackert's house. The trees in her yard were all bare and dark and twisted. The windows of her house looked black and sullen. Just then a cold breeze blew. It bit into my skin. I shuddered.

Cara said, "If you do this one last thing with me, Laura, I'll never bug you about Mrs. Blackert again. I promise." She seemed sincere.

"You really mean it?" I asked.

"I really mean it."

"Okay." I sighed. "I'll do it."

I figured, How bad could it be? We weren't breaking and entering, we weren't going into that awful, creepy dining room, we weren't even spying this time. We were just going to stand on Mrs. Blackert's front stoop, ring the bell, say "Trick or treat," get our candy, and scram. As simple as that.

I wish.

Trick or Treat

Cara had a very determined look on her face as we strode up Mrs. Blackert's front walk. Her lips were pressed together tightly, her eyes stared unblinkingly at Mrs. Blackert's red door, and I noticed that she was strangling her candy bag. Cara was scared! I'd always thought that Cara was fearless, but now I saw, quite clearly, that she was as scared as I was! But she wasn't like me. She couldn't just forget her fear. To conquer it, she had to meet it head on.

We walked up the slate path very slowly. All the leaves at my house had been neatly packed away in bags, but it was clear that no one had raked Mrs. Blackert's yard. Brittle leaves skittered across the path and crunched under our boots.

We climbed up the six brick steps. Before us was Mrs. Blackert's front door. It was huge and forbidding. Thick chunks of muddy red paint hung off it, like scabs.

Cara grabbed the tarnished cat's-head knocker and sent it crashing into the door three times.

Please, I thought, no one be home! Please, don't answer!

But of course the door opened.

In the doorway stood Mrs. Blackert.

She wasn't wearing the black robe with the gold embroidery, as I'd expected. She was wearing a white smock, which was splattered with paint, and her white hair was brushed back into a braid. There was a funny smell about her too. It burned my nose. I recognized the odor from art class—it was paint thinner. Despite her disheveled appearance she was smiling. Mrs. Blackert was happy to see us.

"Trick-or-treaters?" she asked, in her high, crisp English voice.

Both Cara and I nodded. I realized that we'd both forgotten to say those magical words "Trick or treat" when she opened the door.

"Well, let me get you a treat then. Would you young witches care to come inside?" She chuckled.

Quickly, before Cara could even blink an eye, I shook my head. I shook it so violently that my witch's hat almost fell off. I'd vowed never to set foot in that house again. Standing on that stoop was bad enough.

"As you wish," she chirped. "But don't go away! I have something very special . . ." Her voice disappeared with her into the dark house. But I thought I heard her say, "Just for you."

"Let's beat it," I said to Cara. I was so frightened that I'd begun to hiccup.

"Let's see what her treat is," replied Cara. "If it's an apple or something, we can throw it and run away. Whatever it is, we won't eat it!"

"I certainly hope not!" cried a voice—Mrs. Blackert's

voice, I realized with a shock. How had she returned so quickly, so quietly? "Because the trick is that my treat isn't something you eat!"

Between her small, paint-splattered hands was a big squarish object, which was covered with a sheet. Before we could say or do anything, Mrs. Blackert pulled away the sheet and let it drop to the ground. My flesh turned to ice when I saw what she held. It was a painting—a very good portrait of Cara. Oddly enough, in the portrait Cara was wearing a tall black hat. But it wasn't your typical witch's hat, because the brim poked out of only one side. When I inspected the portrait more closely, I saw that the witch's hat was actually Cara's old baseball cap, the one she'd lost a couple of weeks ago in Mrs. Blackert's house. Mrs. Blackert had elongated the top of the cap so that it looked like a sort of witch's baseball hat! In the painting Cara was wearing something else that she'd lost in Mrs. Blackert's house—her old glasses, the round ones with the gold frames. She was holding the handle of a long wooden spoon, stirring something in a big black pot.

I turned and ran down the cement steps, my arms spread out wide, like a bird's wings, my candy bag flapping in the wind. I was flying down the leaf-strewn path when I realized that something was terribly wrong. It was too quiet on that path. My ears should've been filled with the sound of feet, both mine and Cara's, crackling, crunching and shuffling through the leaves, but it was only my solitary footsteps I heard.

I stopped running. I stood for a second staring at the street, my body trembling and jerking from the hiccups. I didn't want to turn around. I wanted to run all the way home and throw myself into Mrs. O's warm, gushy arms. But where was Cara? I had to find out what had happened to my best friend!

I turned around very slowly until I faced Mrs. Blackert's front stoop. Cara wasn't there! She wasn't on the stoop! Only her black cat glasses and her plastic candy bag were there, lying on the cold, gray cement.

I had a very sick feeling in my stomach. Mrs. Blackert stood in the doorway. She held the painting up so that I could see it.

She cried, "Now we'll see who'll be calling whom a witch!" Then she laughed shrilly.

I knew what had happened to Cara. Cara, the *real* Cara, had become one with her portrait. I don't know how else to say it, but it was true! From within the portrait Cara was staring at me with wide, frightened eyes.

"W-w-why?" My voice surprised me. It spilled out of me, all broken up and choppy because of the hiccups. "Why'd you do that to her?"

Mrs. Blackert stopped laughing and became very serious.

"My dear, your friend got what she was looking

for—trouble! Lots of it. If you're wondering, that's what she's brewing in the black pot! Trouble!" Mrs. Blackert giggled. Clearly she had a strange sense of humor. I glanced at poor Cara. She was just standing there woefully, her hands wrapped about that awful wooden spoon.

Then Mrs. Blackert said, "Better for her to make trouble there, in that painting, than out here." She waved her tiny hands around, indicating that she meant the neighborhood, maybe even the world. She continued, "She snooped around my house. She tried to drown my sweet little Felix. I'm afraid, my dear, that there's no room for bad people in this world. But there's plenty of room for them on my walls!" She laughed again.

"But Cara isn't bad," I argued, again surprising myself.

"I'm afraid I disagree. My opinion of her, which was not high to begin with, plunged the day I saw her trying to help that monstrous husband of mine. Bad people stick together. And my husband is the worst. He is a brute. A fiend. In fact I have quite a collection of brutes and fiends on my wall. Now I have another little monster to gaze upon." Mrs. Blackert smiled, somewhat fondly I thought, at her portrait of Cara.

"Cara's not a monster!" I insisted, hot tears streaming down my cheeks. "She's just . . . she's just . . ."

But Mrs. Blackert slammed the door in my face.

Answers in the Universe

I blinked stupidly at Mrs. Blackert's flaky red door for several minutes. Then I bent down and scooped up Cara's candy bag. It was a plastic bag, the kind you get at the grocery store. On it, in green letters, were the words "Health Mart All-Natural Foods." Normally I would've laughed, because nothing in that bag was natural. It was stuffed with Milk Duds, Hershey's bars, and candy corn. But I wasn't in the mood to laugh. Next I picked up Cara's new cat glasses. I held them up to my eyes. Through their thick, smudgy lenses everything appeared very small and faraway. I liked the world this way—it seemed so harmless. I slipped the glasses into Cara's candy bag.

I trudged home. Though I was cold, I didn't go into my house right away. I went into the backyard. It was desolate. The pool had been emptied and covered, and most of the lawn furniture had been stashed away. Two chairs had been left on the patio. I sat in one made of wrought iron—its metal bones had soaked up the cold. I took off my witch's hat and placed it on the slate. I leaned back in the chair and stared up at the twilight sky.

"What am I going to do?" I asked the stars.

I contemplated marching off to the police station and confessing what had happened. The trouble was, *it was crazy.* Too crazy. Why would the police believe a kid like me? And if I told them the truth, I ran the risk of angering Mrs. Blackert. If this happened, she might put me in a painting too. Then who'd save Cara?

My thoughts were like eels, slippery and dark, coiling themselves around my brain, strangling it. What would I say to Cara's father? He was such a sweet, harmless man. How could I lie to him? And yet, how could I tell him the truth?

All I knew was that I was in this alone. I had to save Cara by myself. But how on Earth was I going to get Mrs. Blackert to listen to me?

I sighed, my breath frosty in the cool evening air. Above me the sky was silvery, sparkling.

"The universe has all the answers, Laura." Mrs. O had spoken these words several years ago, when I'd asked her what I should do about all those obnoxious boys. Back then that statement had made absolutely no sense. In fact, it'd hardly seemed like an answer at all. Now I wondered if there was actually some truth in that saying.

I examined the stars. They were strong and bright and clear, and yet they also looked delicate, shimmery, and very, very small. But I knew that their small size was just an illusion. In reality the stars were quite large. Some of those glittering dots I was calling stars were actually planets that were bigger than Earth.

Perhaps if I were like those stars, seemingly small, innocent, and pleasing, yet actually strong and steadfast, Mrs. Blackert might listen to me. If there was one thing I'd learned by now, it was that Mrs. Blackert didn't like bullies.

I rose from the chair and plodded toward the house, realizing that while I didn't have a plan, I at least had a foundation for a plan.

That was a start.

Stories

I told everyone the exact same story I told Mr. Hadaway: On Halloween Cara and I had had a fight, after which she stormed off, leaving me to trick-or-treat alone. I hated lying like that, but the way I saw it, I didn't have much of a choice. I didn't tell a soul the unbelievable truth, and I hid her candy bag and glasses in an old Scrabble box, which I stashed in my closet.

Cara's disappearance created quite a stir. And for a while I was very busy giving interviews to policemen and reporters. The story was splattered across all the papers, and one night it was even featured on the news. I went to our local television station, where they slopped some makeup on my face and sat me under white-hot lights. The newscasters asked the same old stupid questions I'd been asked a hundred times before. I rattled off the same old stupid lies. Mr. Hadaway was sitting right next to me, his haggard face all orange and shiny with makeup. And believe it or not, next to him sat Nimbo. They'd given him a bath.

Throughout the TV segment they kept flashing snapshots of Cara, and they even showed a video she'd made of herself and Nimbo. We saw Cara urging Nimbo to do a few silly tricks she'd taught him. He slaps Cara with his paw, plays dead, and he even dances around a little. I have to say, for an old dog he wasn't too bad. I remembered that when she made that video, about a year ago, she planned to send it in to some TV show. She never did. And now here it was on the national news.

I had my mother tape the segment. I knew it was something Cara wouldn't want to miss. She always wanted to be famous.

Mr. Hadaway

On Wednesday a week before Thanksgiving I visited Mr. Hadaway. To tell you the truth, I was kind of worried about him. He certainly wasn't the luckiest man in the world, what with his wife dying and daughter missing. It occurred to me that it might do him some good if he started carrying around a charm, like a rabbit's foot or a four-leaf clover, because when you got right down to it, Mr. Hadaway needed all the luck he could get.

So I dropped by the cottage to see if he was okay. He wasn't. His hair looked an awful lot like Nimbo's ears—

long and scraggly. His eyes were all wet and bloodshot, and he'd lost weight I hadn't even known he'd had. Everything about him was faded and rumpled, like he'd been through the washing machine too many times.

"Hi, Mr. Hadaway!" I said, forcing my voice to sound chipper and bright.

He gestured me to come inside. Surprisingly, it was very neat. Usually research papers, lecture notes, and open books were scattered across the floor. You had to be very careful where you stepped. You didn't want to leave a shoe print on someone's thesis. But, except for an old, weathered photo album, which lay open on a table, everything had been put away.

I sat in a chair opposite Mr. Hadaway and rummaged through my mind for something to say.

Finally, I cleared my throat and said the only thing I could think of: "Mr. Hadaway," I began, "what's new?" After I said those words, I wished I could take them back—they sounded so pathetically dumb!

Mr. Hadaway shook his disheveled head. "Tonight there's a lunar eclipse, but I probably won't watch it. It just wouldn't be the same without . . . well, you know. Last Saturday there was a march to save the Philippine seahorses," he continued in this weary voice. "But I didn't go." He lifted his hands, gave a great big sigh, then let them fall back into his lap. "And I never go to the movies anymore. I don't dare. I try not to leave the

119

cottage at all. You never know—the police might call with some information, or . . ." He glanced anxiously toward the entrance.

I tried to tell Mr. Hadaway that I knew, *I just knew,* that Cara was going to turn up. I thought that might cheer him a bit, but he barely even listened to me. He just sat there in this big old armchair staring into space the whole time I talked.

Finally he looked me right in the eye and said, "It's my fault she left."

"What?" I asked, amazed. It'd never occurred to me that he thought Cara had run away.

"It's all that macrobiotic food I made her eat. Those dried beans," he told me. "Cara hated them. Washed them down with water, like they were vitamin pills. It was the only way she could eat them." His glasses fogged noticeably.

"Look, Mr. Hadaway," I said, "I happen to know for a fact that Cara loved you very much and she didn't really mind all those beans and grains and funny juices."

"You think so?" he asked, his eyes hopeful.

I nodded.

But when I turned around at the door to say good-bye to him, he looked just as despondent as before. I guess no one could've made him feel better—no one, that is, but Cara.

Before I went home, I visited Nimbo in his dirt hole. I knew that Cara would want me to give him a good old scratch behind the ears. If there's one thing Nimbo loved, it was an ear scratch. He was always getting mites in his ears, which made them itch.

Nimbo looked miserable too. He'd always been a chubby sort of dog—Cara had put him on about a million diets—but now he was all bones and droopy eyes, just like Mr. Hadaway. He wouldn't even get out of his dirt hole to greet me. He just looked up at me with his poor, afflicted eyes, then turned his gaze back to the cottage door. I bet he stayed in that hole all day, although the earth was now cold and hard. I bet he was also waiting for Cara, anticipating the moment she'd fly out the back door of the cottage, his leash swinging in her hand.

While I scratched his ears, I pieced together my plan. I knew *what* I wanted to say to Mrs. Blackert; I just wasn't sure *how* to get her to listen to me. I couldn't simply knock on Mrs. Blackert's door and blab away about Cara's virtues. Maybe I should bring her some sort of gift or peace offering, something to break the ice, but what?

After about ten minutes I left Nimbo and the cottage and headed off for home. I was walking along the sidewalk, wrangling with my plan, when I practically bumped right into Greg Mox. He was sitting on his bike directly in my path, his basket loaded with newspapers. He curled his thin lips over his eyeteeth and snarled at me, just like a wolf.

Greg Mox

Greg Mox was bigger than I remembered. Either I'd shrunk or he'd grown. The way things had been going lately, anything was possible. His eyes looked smaller and meaner, like two hard pieces of gravel. He was chewing gum.

My limbs felt light and quivery, like feathers. I stood there wishing they were feathers, wishing I could fly.

"Where's Four Eyes?" Mox jeered. "I hear she's gone. Disappeared just like that!" He snapped his fingers.

I cleared my throat. I didn't want my voice to sound wobbly and weak. When Cara spoke to Mox, her voice never shook. It was always strong and forceful, like a train barreling down the tracks.

I said, "You heard right." I tried to smile, but my lips didn't quite make it. They twitched a bit, then sort of got stuck.

"If you ask me, Laura, it's good riddance!" He made a series of smacking noises with his gum.

"I didn't ask you." Where had those words come from?

"What'd you say?" He leaned over his bicycle so that his face was dangerously close to mine. I could feel his breath, hot and moist, against my cheeks. It smelled of cherry-flavored gum.

"You heard me," I said. I was struggling now to stay in control.

"This gum is getting a little stale, Laura," Mox snarled, removing the slimy red gob from his mouth. "I don't want it anymore. Nice guy that I am, I'm gonna share it with you. 'Cause I know how you like to wear it in your hair!" He let loose brays and neighs of awful horse laughter.

I don't know what came over me. I really don't. All I know is that I felt this enormous surge of energy, as though a geyser had sprung forth within me. I reached out with both hands and gave Mox's newspaper basket a hearty shove. Then I kicked his bicycle wheel so hard my toes throbbed.

Mox gave me a startled look before crashing to the ground like a giant bowling pin. His bicycle and newspapers fell on top of him.

"See you later, Mox Pox!" I shouted.

And I tore down the street.

Tacos

I was exhilarated! I couldn't believe what I'd done. I burst into the house and stared at myself in the hall mirror. Surprisingly I looked the same. There was the same oval face, the same pale-blue eyes. But I *was* different, I knew I was. Deep within me something had changed.

All at once I was overcome by a desire to call Cara. I wanted to tell her everything that'd just happened. But of course I couldn't. I knew better than anyone else that Cara was nowhere near a phone.

My parents weren't home, and Lucy was on the phone, so I wandered into the kitchen to share my victory with Mrs. O.

When I was through telling her my tale, Mrs. O cried, "I always knew that underneath that shy façade, you were a little dynamo, Laura!" She looked pretty thrilled. One way or another she was always rooting for me.

She said, "Why don't we have a celebratory feast? How about some tacos?"

Tacos?

I stared at her, but I didn't see her at all. All I could see was that word, "tacos," banging around in my head.

Tacos—why hadn't I thought of them before? Mrs. Blackert had mentioned them that first night we saw her in her dining room. And then Mr. Deever had mentioned them again, telling us how much Mrs. Blackert loved to eat them.

"Laura, did I say something wrong?" Mrs. O asked. She peered worriedly into my face.

"No!" I practically shouted. "Tacos are a great idea!"

What I didn't say was that they were also the missing part of my plan! Tacos would be my peace offering, my gift to Mrs. Blackert.

Taco making is an art, it really is. I suppose you can be boring and just make a couple of ingredients, but Mrs. O and I never do that. We whip up about a million different things, which we spread all over the table, so everyone in the family can stuff their own shells.

I cooked the ground meat in a little bit of garlic and butter while Mrs. O chopped the tomatoes, onions, peppers, and lettuce. Mrs. O never let me slice or chop. She said that the way I daydream, I'd probably hack off a finger. But I didn't mind cooking the meat. I liked listening to it hiss and snap. I liked watching it change from pink to brown.

While the meat sizzled, I thought about my plan. It was a good plan, I knew it; still, it made me nervous. But every time I thought I'd chicken out, I recalled the look of disbelief on Mox's face when I pushed him over. His slack, stunned mouth, his widened eyes—those images empowered me.

"I can do it," I muttered, recalling how ridiculous Mox had looked under that heap of newspapers. "I know I can."

"Do what, Laura?" Mrs. O looked up from her minced tomato.

"Beat Mary Jane next year in the tournament."

Mrs. O studied me carefully. Then she furrowed her brow. "Of course you can," she said. "You can do anything if you just set your mind to it."

When we were through cooking and chopping, and had set everything out in little bowls on the table, I started stuffing two tacos. I hoped that Mrs. Blackert wasn't fussy.

"Laura, aren't you going to wait till dinnertime?" Mrs. O asked. She had just finished buttoning her tweed coat and was adjusting her crumpled velvet hat, which had a flower plastered on the side. Whenever she wore it, she reminded me of a plumper, older Mary Poppins.

"I'm going to bring these to Mr. Hadaway," I told her. "He's gotten awfully skinny."

"Just be sure to leave your mother a note, so she doesn't worry." She ruffled my hair, then waddled out the door. A few minutes later I heard the rumble of her little car.

The Visit

When I could no longer hear Mrs. O's car, I pulled on my fuzzy pink gloves, slipped into my purple parka, and stepped outside. But I didn't turn toward the cottage. I walked in the direction of Mrs. Blackert's house, tightly clutching my taco bag.

Though it wasn't even five fifteen, it was already dark.

I noticed that the moon was full. It loomed out of the blackness like a big white eye. Around the moon, like a hazy shadow, was an eerie orange mist. The street was empty except for me.

My nerves felt like tight springs, coiling and uncoiling, bouncing and jangling around. Each time my feet crunched on a dead leaf, I jumped.

When I reached Mrs. Blackert's house, I stared at her slate path, which seemed longer than I remembered, endless. At the end of the path, looming ominously, daring me to approach, was Mrs. Blackert's sinister door.

I gripped the tacos more tightly. They were still warm from the cooked meat. There was something comforting about that warmth, some reminder of a bright, homey kitchen filled with savory smells and the jolly girth of Mrs. O.

I walked along the slate path carefully, trying to be quiet, trying not to step on stray leaves. Every now and then my eyes slid to either side of the path, examining the trees, making sure that that awful ivy was still coiled around them, making sure it wasn't slithering after me. When I was halfway to the door, something skulked out of the darkness. It was long and lean and low to the ground. A cat, I realized, a cold, prickly horror taking hold of me. One of Mrs. Blackert's cats!

I stopped walking.

I stood perfectly still.

The cat seated itself in the middle of the path, staring at me with radiant eyes, gnashing its jagged white teeth.

I swallowed hard. Walk around it, I told myself. It's just a cat. But soon the solitary cat was joined by another cat, and then another. Soon the path was lined with cats, sitting with their tails curling and uncurling, their mouths opening menacingly, their eyes burning holes through the night.

Get out of here, a little voice cried within me. Go home. I pictured our cozy den with its wooden walls and plush red rug. I pictured the bright flashes of the TV and the warm orange glow of the lamps, and I was filled with an aching desire to be there, in that room, huddled in a chair. But then I felt the weight in my hand, the weight of the two tacos I'd stuffed and wrapped for Mrs. Blackert, and I knew I couldn't go home. Only a chicken would do that, and as I'd proved today when I'd toppled Greg Mox, I was no longer a chicken. I had a mission to accomplish.

I stepped off the path, to the left of the cats. I closed my eyes and moved my feet over the wilted grass. I expected to hear a chorus of hisses. I expected to feel the sharp sting of four dozen paws' worth of claws. But nothing happened.

I shuffled along blindly for what seemed like hours, until I tripped over Mrs. Blackert's stoop and fell flat on my face. My knees, elbows, and forehead smashed into the hard brick steps. I moaned. The taco bag slipped from my hand.

I lay for several seconds, stunned and dazed, and then a current of horror ran through me. The cats! I had to get up before they pounced on me and tore me and my tacos to shreds!

I grabbed the bag and rose to my feet. Slowly, fearfully, I peered over my shoulder. There, about a foot away, sat the cats. They had formed a huddle, and all their eyes—their luminous feline eyes—were fixed on me.

I placed a quivering hand on the cold, brass cat's-head knocker and struck the door. The sound clattered through the night. It was almost as loud as my heart.

Laura the Courageous

Before I could take my hand off the brass ring, the door flew open, and there was Mrs. Blackert.

She cried, "Why, Laura, what a pleasant surprise!" Slung about her neck was the fat cat with the red-tipped tail. Felix, I thought, recalling that day by the pool. Above her ebony robe, Mrs. Blackert's wavy white hair floated like sea foam. Peering out of her ivory face, like two black, bottomless pits, were her eyes. They were the blackest things I'd ever seen, blacker even than the night, which was quickly closing in on me.

"Please, come inside," she said. The time for turning back had passed.

I stepped into Mrs. Blackert's house. One by one the orange cats followed me, brushing against my leg.

I entered a rather large foyer. The only light came from a candle, which sat on a table in front of a mirror. The flame shuddered when Mrs. Blackert shut the door. Her face, half in the shadows and half in the candle's pale-yellow glow, looked both lively and fierce.

"I must say I was not expecting *you*, Laura," she said with a slow smile. Her lipstick was very dark. I liked the red shade better. This color, like her eyes, invited you to fall into an abyss from which you might never crawl out. "When Felix told me you were outside, I was terribly surprised. I was under the impression that courage was not one of your strong points."

I guess it was that crisp, insulting, slightly mocking voice of hers that gave me the nerve to speak. I cleared my throat. I looked her right in the eye and said, as evenly as I could, "I wanted to talk to you about something, Mrs. Blackert."

"Oh, how marvelous! A chat, we're to have a chat! You and I!" She tucked her hands underneath her chin so that they formed a sort of white ribbon. Then she said, "Let's chat in the dining room, shall we? I believe you like it in there."

Her feet, clad in what looked like black ballet slippers, pitter-pattered down a dark hallway.

An Offering

The dining room was just as I'd remembered it. Candles blazed, the oriental rug adorned the floor, heavy drapes framed the windows, and of course the portraits still hung on the wall.

My eyes roved the room frantically, searching for Cara. When I saw her, I gasped. She was hanging right next to Doug Hirst III! She was still dressed like a witch. She was still stirring trouble in a big black pot. Her eyes looked bigger than I remembered, and her face was thinner, paler, sadder. To reassure her, and perhaps to reassure myself, I tried to smile, but my lips wouldn't move. Despite my best efforts they remained grimly locked together.

Mrs. Blackert said, "Please, my dear, take off your coat and gloves and stay awhile."

The cats positioned themselves all over the room, like guards. Reluctantly, I hung my parka on the back of one of the dining-room chairs. I pulled off my gloves and stuffed them into the parka's pockets. Then I sat down.

An open bottle of champagne, a bowl of tortilla chips, and a jar of salsa were before me on the dining-room table.

Mrs. Blackert said, "I was just having supper, dear. Chips with salsa and a touch of champagne. Can I pour you a glass?"

I shook my head. "No thank you. I'm not allowed to have alcoholic beverages." I added, "I'm only twelve."

I guess a lot of kids would've accepted her offer, but I'm not big on fizzy, bubbly drinks. Believe it or not, I don't even like soda. Besides, I couldn't help thinking that maybe there was some evil potion in the champagne to put me under Mrs. Blackert's spell.

"That's a lot of bloody rot! *I* drank champagne when *I* was twelve," scoffed Mrs. Blackert. She threw her head back and took a big swig from her glass, almost emptying it.

I got the funny feeling that her twelve and my twelve weren't exactly the same, so I blurted, "Mrs. Blackert, how old are you?"

"Laura!" she exclaimed. "Didn't your mother ever tell you it is impolite to ask a lady her age?"

I nodded. She most certainly had. My mother was a real stickler about manners. But as I said, I got the feeling that when it came to Mrs. Blackert, age didn't matter. I was right.

She said, "However, since you ask, I am four hundred fifty years old." She giggled rather girlishly. "I have aged rather well, wouldn't you say?"

I was completely dumbstruck. The funny thing was, I believed her.

"Calm yourself, dear, and close that mouth of yours. I do not enjoy staring at your teeth. We witches age quite differently from you mortals, fortunately for us." Her eyes flitted to the portrait of her decrepit husband, as if to emphasize this point.

Mrs. Blackert took a chip, dipped it into the jar of salsa, then bit into it daintily. She waited till she swallowed before she spoke. "Now that we have had our chat, why don't you give me a little something of yours so that we can get this over with? Your purple parka perhaps?" She grinned.

I stared at her in horror.

"No need to look so worried, dear. I promise that once I have done a lovely portrait of you, I will hang you right next to your chum Cara."

I glanced at Cara. Her eyebrows had risen above her glasses and she was chomping on her nails.

Mrs. Blackert rose. For a moment, as though a breeze had suddenly swept through the dining room, her hair and her robe lifted into the air and rippled behind her. But there was no breeze in the room. It was deathly still. Mrs. Blackert stepped toward me threateningly, her arms stretched forward, her hands crawling toward me like hungry white spiders. She said, her voice low and unmistakably evil, "You did not think I would simply let you chat and leave, did you?"

I shrank farther back in my seat, my mouth too dry for speech. Dimly, I was aware that I had to act. If I didn't, there was a very good chance I might never leave this frightening house.

With a great effort I said, "Mrs. Blackert, I brought you something." I lifted the bag of tacos and held them out to her. "Tacos," I sputtered.

Mrs. Blackert froze. For one long, agonizing moment she merely stared at me. Then she snatched the bag and peered inside. She pulled out one of the tacos I'd wrapped in tinfoil and sniffed it. Her whole face changed then. Her mouth softened, and the creases around her mouth and eyes disappeared.

"Mmm . . ." she said, throwing back her hoary head. "Divine." She unwrapped the taco and took a big bite. As she chewed—rather noisily, I thought—her eyelids closed halfway. She looked perfectly blissful.

I stayed in my seat, my heart pounding, praying the taco tasted especially good.

After several more hearty bites Mrs. Blackert declared happily, "This is simply scrumptious."

A great big sigh rattled through me like a freight train. For the moment Mrs. Blackert and her grabby little hands seemed more interested in the taco than in me, which meant that now was my chance to say what

I'd planned. I took a deep breath, then began, "There's another taco in the bag. I brought them to show you that I mean well, Mrs. Blackert. All I want is the chance to ask you to please, please let Cara go."

I told Mrs. Blackert about Cara's dad—how skinny he'd grown and how rotten things had been for him, with Cara gone and her mother having died years ago. Then I told her about Nimbo, and how he stayed out in the cold all day long, refusing to leave his dirt hole. I described how good Cara had been to Nimbo. How she'd rescued him from an animal shelter and fattened him up. I emphasized that I was worried about Mr. Hadaway and Nimbo, afraid that without Cara they wouldn't make it through the winter. I tossed in a lot of soppy adjectives and embellished like crazy, because if there was one thing I'd learned from our meeting with Mr. Deever, it was that Mrs. Blackert definitely had a big, gushy soft spot somewhere in her withered heart. If I was lucky, it was still there.

"Mrs. Blackert," I pleaded, "please free Cara. Sure, you painted a very good portrait of her, but you did so without really seeing the whole Cara!"

I studied Mrs. Blackert to see if my words had any effect. She didn't respond right away. She just sat silently in her chair, stroking Felix. Somewhere outside, a dog let out a long, wolfish howl. I imagined it was Nimbo, adding his two cents, begging Mrs. Blackert to set Cara free. I glanced at the portraits. All their faces were fixed upon Mrs. Blackert, their eyes wide with anticipation. After what felt like hours she said slowly, "I admire your courage, Laura. Actually, I am rather astounded by it. But . . ." Her voice drifted off. Felix began to purr.

Mrs. Blackert smiled tenderly at the big, rumbling lump of fur in her lap. For a brief moment it transformed her face, softening it, and I caught a glimpse of the woman Mrs. Blackert must've once been. Then the smile was gone. In its place was a hard, bitter scowl, which Mrs. Blackert directed at Cara. She barked angrily, "I do not trust that little imp. She was extraordinarily cruel to my sweet little Felix."

Cara was about to deliver a damaging torrent of words, but all she managed to say was "But . . ." before I turned to her and pressed my fingers to my lips. I knew that if she uttered another peep, she'd never leave that portrait. Cara might've been the toughest kid on our block, but she certainly didn't know how to handle Mrs. Blackert.

"Mrs. Blackert," I said earnestly, before she could comment on Cara's brief and sudden outburst, "Cara is wild about animals. All animals. It's just that over the summer she read this crazy witch book, and afterward she mistakenly believed that your cats were evil."

"Those bloody witch books!" sneered Mrs. Blackert.

"They get everything wrong!" She surveyed the room, eyeing her cats. Then she said to them, "What do you think, my sweets—should I free her?" She pointed to Cara.

Together the cats' orange heads turned toward Cara. They studied her with their strange, candlelit eyes.

Oh no, I thought, my hopes evaporating. There was no way those cats were going to tell Mrs. Blackert to free Cara. Not after she'd thrown Felix into the pool. Cara was doomed!

The whole room began to purr. It sounded as though a lot of miniature lawn mowers were skimming over the carpet, zipping around the dining room. The purring was so loud that very softly, almost imperceptibly, my chair began to vibrate.

Suddenly, my chair was still, and the room was dead silent. The cats' verdict was in.

Mrs. Blackert nodded her white head slowly, then turned to me. I tried to read the cats' answer in her expression, but I couldn't. All I could see was that Mrs. Blackert looked quite mad—and I don't mean angry. What had those cats told her?

"It's your lucky day today, Laura," Mrs. Blackert said, just when the suspense seemed unbearable, "because my precious kitties have told me to set Cara free."

"They have?" I was truly shocked.

"They have. You see, my dear, despite what your friend did to Felix, they were touched by how kind she's been to her mangy old dog, what's-his-name."

"Nimbo," I told her.

"Yes. Well, it appears that for quite some time my cats have been watching her. They saw how she played with that old mongrel, brushed the snarls out of his shaggy coat, cleaned his mite-infested ears. They say that anyone who could be as nice as she was to that poor, enfeebled creature could not possibly be all that bad. They say he needs her."

I smiled nervously at those crazy orange cats. I'd underestimated them.

"Of course I will only release her on one condition."

My heart sank. "What's that?"

"I will keep her glasses and her hat. If she snoops around here again, or does anything to arouse my attention, back into the portrait she goes."

Mrs. Blackert rose and walked over to Cara's portrait.

"Please, let me go too!" moaned Hirst. He clasped his gnarly hands together and widened his beady bird eyes.

Mrs. Blackert glared at Hirst and shouted, her voice so shrill it stung my ears, "If I hear another peep out of you, I will paint a big black panther into that picture! One with fangs and claws as sharp as daggers! And you will be its supper. How would you like that?"

"No! Please! I beg of you!" Hirst blubbered. As he shrank farther into the portrait, Mrs. Blackert smiled at him. It was a terrible, inhuman, witch's smile.

The Coaxing Voices

Very carefully Mrs. Blackert lifted Cara's portrait off the wall.

"Stay here, sweeties," Mrs. Blackert told the cats. She explained, "I do not let them upstairs because of their fur—it gets into my paints."

Mrs. Blackert snatched one of the black candles from the table. Holding the candle in one hand and Cara's portrait in the other, she hurried out of the room. I followed her. The cats remained on the dining-room rug, licking their paws, twirling their stringy orange tails.

I was trotting after Mrs. Blackert when all of a sudden she stopped walking. She came to a complete standstill. Luckily, tennis had made me quick on my feet, or I would've crashed right into her. While I danced about unsteadily, Mrs. Blackert whirled around to face me.

"Not so fast, my dear," she hissed. I froze. "You cannot possibly think I would let *you* see my secret workroom?" Her laughter stabbed the silence. "No, dear, absolutely no one enters my workroom but me. You must remain down here with the cats. Help yourself to some chips and salsa. Leave Cara to me." Then she spun about and disappeared with Cara up a long, dark staircase.

I stood in her unlit living room watching the glow of her candle fade. When the last of that murky yellow light slipped upstairs, I retraced my steps into the dining room. I stared sullenly at the chips and salsa on the table. Chips and salsa—humph! My stomach was so jumpy, I couldn't eat a bite.

I was contemplating those chips when all of a sudden a slimy, conniving voice said, "I wouldn't trust her if I were you, Laura. Witches are infamous liars. Why, I bet at this very moment that disgusting old hag is turning your Cara into a worm or a toad." Doug Hirst III grinned at me. His voice was so slick and enticing, I found it impossible to ignore. "The last person she took into that secret room of hers was this old geezer by the name of Hilb, Carl Hilb. You wouldn't believe what happened to him!"

I felt the blood drain out of my face. I remembered that name. Carl Hilb! He was the pesky reporter Cara had told me about! The one she'd referred to as a barnacle! The one who had mysteriously disappeared years ago!

Hirst said, "One day that ogress lugged Hilb's portrait home. Got it out of some museum in Massachusetts. She hung the old goat in here, on the wall, with the rest of us. Hilb was a typical reporter—a regular blabbermouth. I tell you, he never shut up. 'Please let me go! Please let me out!' Yak, yak, yak, day and night.

One cold evening he pushed her too far. Got on her nerves. Beastly old witch that she is, she took him upstairs to her secret room, and guess what she did."

I stared at him questioningly.

Hirst licked his thin white lips. "She painted an alligator into the portrait with him. Biggest gator I've ever seen. For a couple of days the alligator just watched Hilb. But I knew his days were numbered. Each morning, when the sun rose, the gator's mouth was opened a little bit wider. Then one day I saw right into its gullet, and what a frightening sight that was! Its teeth just hung there like icicles, a piercing gateway to an endless black pit. That night the gator ate old Hilb. Gobbled him up. I didn't see it happen, because it was pitifully black in here, but I could hear the screams. The next day Hilb wasn't staring out of the portrait as usual. The only thing in the painting was the gator. It just sat there with an enormous bulge in its gut!"

The other portraits giggled. "It's true!" several of them hollered.

I felt horribly ill. What if Mrs. Blackert did that to Cara? What if she painted some horrible monster into that portrait with her? What if she made me watch while it ate her up?

Then I had another awful thought. What if, right this very minute, she was painting a portrait of me? How fast could she whip those things out? And what belongings of mine did she have? I checked the dining-room chair to see if my purple parka was still there. It was.

"When it comes to that vicious old witch, anything is possible," Hirst stated.

Despite my dislike of him, I almost agreed. Mrs. Blackert did have an awfully odd sense of humor.

"If I were you, Laura, I'd spy on her," Inspector Mete said.

"Yeah," Snake Eyes chimed in. "If you want to save your friend, you better hurry on up there and see what that rotten old lady is up to!"

"If you don't, you may never see Cara again," Hirst added solemnly.

I didn't trust those portraits. Still, I couldn't help thinking they were right. Cara's rescue was my responsibility. She was relying on me, and so were Nimbo and Mr. Hadaway. At the very least, I reasoned, I should check to see if Mrs. Blackert was keeping her word.

The cats were watching me with their wise yellow eyes. One wrong move out of me and they'd pounce, scratch, and bite! I sighed. There was no way I could sneak after Mrs. Blackert.

Then I had an idea. A thrilling, frightening idea. An idea that depended on the contents of Mrs. Blackert's refrigerator.

"Hmm," I mused aloud for the benefit of those enchanted cats, "I'd sure like to have a glass of juice with those chips. I'll see if Mrs. Blackert has some." I attempted a bright smile, then waltzed off toward the kitchen. One by one, the cats followed behind me.

There were no lights on in the kitchen. The kitchen was as black as Mrs. Blackert's eyes. I groped around, trying to remember if and where I'd seen a refrigerator almost two months ago, when Cara and I had sneaked through the house. My hands dipped into a perfectly dry sink basin, darted over a cold stove, and skimmed over a smooth kitchen table before reaching something tall and rectangular. I felt the handle, heard the familiar hum. I pulled it open.

A little light flicked on. There wasn't much in that fridge—a moldy hunk of cheese, some droopy green grapes, another bottle of champagne. Finally I found what I was looking for—caviar! I grabbed that hideous jar and yanked it out of the fridge.

"Look!" I said to the glowing eyes around me. "Caviar!" Purring, loud and insistent, filled the room. I hurried back into the dining room. I prayed my plan would work.

I dumped the tortilla chips all over the table. Next I opened that putrid jar of fish eggs and plopped them into the emptied porcelain bowl, hitting the bottom of the jar with my hand several times in an effort to free each and every slimy morsel. Soon the bowl was filled with a lumpy black mound, and the dining room reeked of salt and fish. The cats were purring so loudly, I was afraid Mrs. Blackert might hear them.

I moved away from the bowl. The cats, all of them, pounced on it.

"Good work, Laura," Hirst whispered.

While the cats devoured their vile feast, I ran out of the dining room, through the living room, and up the stairs after Mrs. Blackert.

"Please don't let me be too late!" I whispered.

Uncasting a Spell

The upstairs was as black as the kitchen. I never would've known where to go if it hadn't been for the candlelight. A yellow glow beckoned from a room to my left. Slowly, stealthily, my heart beating so loudly I feared it would give me away, I followed it.

I tiptoed delicately, stopping only when I reached a room with tall, rectangular windows that were separated by very thin strips of wood.

Mrs. Blackert stood hunched over. Her curved back, now swathed in the white smock, faced me. Cara's portrait rested in front of her on an easel. Around them both, a zillion candles blazed. The candlelight and the shimmering white moon accentuated the shadows of the trees outside. When the wind blew, the gnarly shadows dipped toward one another, then drew apart, as if they were engaged in some sort of dance. My eyes rose to the columns of windows. In the glass were ghostly images. People dressed in capes and gowns whirled about frantically. Goats and cats and cows appeared to be standing at their feet.

Everything in the room seemed to be enchanted. Besides the dancing shadows and the whirling ghosts, I saw clear jars filled with what looked like potions of the most brilliant hues. The potions threw off beams of color, which cast a rainbow on the shadow-filled floor.

Hanging from a tall metal rack were paintbrushes with bristles as white as Mrs. Blackert's hair. Slumped against one another on the floor were quite a few large blank canvases.

All of a sudden Mrs. Blackert turned. If I hadn't been watching her so intently, she surely would've caught me peeking at her from the doorway. But I was able to duck into the shadows just in time to escape her seething midnight gaze.

There was some clinking and shuffling; then I heard her exclaim, "Aha! This should do the trick!"

When I peered into the room again, I saw that Mrs. Blackert had her back to me. Grasped in her hand was a clear jar. At first I thought the jar was empty, but then I realized that it was full of a crystalline liquid, which sparkled in the candlelight like diamonds.

Mrs. Blackert placed the jar next to the easel. She

picked up a tendril of her hair—her own white, rippling hair—and dipped the end of it into the jar of clear liquid. Then she bent down and touched her hair to the background of the portrait. Because she was bent over, I could see Cara's face. It was as white as Mrs. Blackert's hair, and her eyes were bulging out of their sockets. I guess she was as petrified as I was.

Miraculously, where Mrs. Blackert's hair touched the canvas, the paint simply faded away, leaving a clean white spot. I stood silently in the doorway, hardly breathing at all, watching her sweep that coated tendril along the canvas, doing a sort of reverse kind of painting. She continued dipping her hair into the crystalline liquid and brushing it along the canvas until, gradually, the paint surrounding Cara completely disappeared.

Clearly Mrs. Blackert wasn't painting a portrait of me, nor was she painting a monster into Cara's portrait. It looked as if she was, indeed, freeing Cara!

Please hurry, I silently begged her. Time was of the essence. You see, I hadn't forgotten about those cats. Surely they'd finished the caviar by now. Once they realized that I'd fled up the forbidden stairway, there was no telling what they might do!

It occurred to me that the smart thing for *me* to do was to creep back down the stairs. It was possible that those caviar-crazed cats hadn't yet noticed my absence.

If I retreated now, I might have enough time to hide the caviar jar and put the tortilla chips back in the bowl before Mrs. Blackert returned. Then, when she did appear, I could pretend I'd been in the dining room all along. This would've been the intelligent thing to do.

But I didn't do it. I was transfixed, mesmerized by the magic unfolding before me.

Mrs. Blackert swept her enchanted hair around and around the canvas. When Cara stood in the white background, the strangest thing I've ever seen happened.

Cara grew.

Right before my eyes she swelled and enlarged until she wasn't in the canvas at all. Rather, she hovered before Mrs. Blackert like a specter.

All at once, she was standing on that shadowy floor.

That's when the inevitable happened. I heard a cry— a long, urgent shriek coming from the stairs. This lone cry was followed by a chorus of wails. The cats were letting Mrs. Blackert know I had followed her.

I listened, paralyzed. I hovered in the shadows, my heart heaving against my chest, a prickling sensation running from the back of my ears down my neck. We were caught, nabbed!

Then I pinched myself hard. I twisted the flesh on my arm until the panic subsided a little, leaving me with one blaring thought: Cara and I had to get away from Mrs. Blackert—fast!

"Cara, Run!"

"Cara, run!" I screamed.

I caught only a glimpse of Mrs. Blackert's startled face before Cara darted past her and out the doorway. I followed her on jelly legs, my feet thudding down the stairs, my hand gripping the banister.

I reached the bottom of the stairs just in time to see Cara dodge past the cats toward the front door, her hand pressed to her head. She was holding her hat, making sure it didn't fall into Mrs. Blackert's creative clutches again.

Perhaps it was seeing Cara grab her hat like that that reminded me of the one thing I had almost forgotten: my purple parka! It still hung off the back of the dining-room chair! If I left it behind, I was doomed.

I turned toward the dining room just as Mrs. Blackert reached the top of the stairs. Out of the corner of my eye I saw her lift her arm and point one pale, trembling finger toward Cara. "Seize that girl! Get her hat! Get her glasses! Get *something!*" she screeched to her cats. The cats hurled themselves at the open door like bright-orange cannonballs. Both they and Cara vanished into the night.

I dashed into the dining room, toward the purple swell of my parka.

"I'll get you, Laura!" Mrs. Blackert hollered from the stairs. "You treacherous wretch!"

As I wriggled into my parka, the portraits laughed.

"Nice try, Blondie!" Mete chuckled.

"You really blew it!" Snake Eyes taunted

"You're going to be one of us now, Laura!" Hirst gloated.

And the worst of it was, they were right. They had tricked me into spying on Mrs. Blackert. Probably they'd known all along that I'd get caught. *And now I was trapped.* To reach the front door, I'd have to get past Mrs. Blackert, and I knew she would never allow that.

Behind the Curtains

Mrs. Blackert was in the living room; I could hear the thud of her feet. In several seconds she would be in the dining room—with me.

There was only one thing for me to do: hide. Perhaps Mrs. Blackert would think I had escaped out the front door with Cara. I glanced around the room, my eyes finally alighting upon the red-velvet drapes. There wasn't time to think. I sprinted across the room and slipped behind the heavy, musty curtain folds. The drapes were long and full. They fell past my sneakers, bunching somewhat on the floor. Behind them it was dark.

Against my back the wall and window were ice cold. I was glad I was wearing my parka.

Don't breathe, I told myself. Don't hiccup or twitch a single muscle.

I held my breath and listened. I heard Mrs. Blackert's feet pad into the dining room. My limbs stiffened as, somewhere in the middle of the room, she stopped. Though I could see nothing, I knew she was searching for me.

"Where is she? Where is that bloody creature?" I heard her mutter. Her voice was much uglier than it'd ever been before. It filled me with a sense of impending dread.

"Is it possible that that little trickster escaped out the front?" Mrs. Blackert mused. "Or did the conniving devil slip out the back?"

The back entrance! I had forgotten all about those French doors that opened into Mrs. Blackert's backyard! Had I remembered them, I would've been home by now! I would've been safe. Tears welled up in my eyes.

I heard the rustle of Mrs. Blackert's black robe. My eyes widened, so sure was I that she was coming for me. I envisioned her wrenching apart the curtains, digging her long, black nails into my flesh!

I heard Mrs. Blackert's feet move across the floor—toward the kitchen! She was walking away from me! I felt a surge of hope. When her footsteps were far enough away, I would spring out from behind the curtain and bolt for the front door!

But some things are just not meant to happen.

"That little fool didn't leave the house!" Doug Hirst exploded. To my horror, Mrs. Blackert's footsteps ceased.

"What?" she sputtered.

"You heard me," Hirst snarled.

"Then tell me where she is," Mrs. Blackert demanded. I noticed that her voice sounded closer.

"I will tell you," Hirst said, and I was sure he was smiling his awful, oily smile, "only if you promise to free me afterward."

There was a lengthy pause during which I contemplated making a break for it. But I knew this would be useless. Though I wasn't sure where in the room Mrs. Blackert stood, I knew that wherever she was, she could easily block either of my exits. I had a whole dining-room table to get around before I could go anywhere.

"Promise me," Hirst urged.

"Very well," Mrs. Blackert told him crisply. "I promise."

Gasps flooded the room.

I thought Hirst would give me away right then and there. I imagined him shouting gleefully, "She's behind the curtain!" But what followed was silence.

During those endless minutes I tried to determine what was going on. But that was impossible, because none of the portraits made a sound, and as far as I could tell, Mrs. Blackert stood perfectly still. I couldn't hear the patter of her feet or the swish of her garments.

As each minute passed, I grew increasingly cold. This coldness came from inside me—from some deep inner place—and spread outward toward my skin. I began to shiver.

And then a hand reached around the curtain and, like a snake, wrapped itself around my wrist.

Captured

Surprisingly, despite her relatively small stature, Mrs. Blackert was as strong as an ox. With steely hands she dragged me out of the dining room.

"Hey, what about me?" Hirst called after her. "We had a deal, remember! I pointed her out. Now you owe me!" he yelled.

"Don't you worry," Mrs. Blackert replied, her voice as calm as the sea before a violent storm. "You will get what is coming to you! I promise!"

She hauled me up the stairs as if I were a rag doll and tied me to a chair in her workroom. She bound my wrists behind me with rope and tied my ankles to the legs of the chair.

Then she wagged a finger at me. "If I hear so much as a little squeak from you, I will punish you severely," she warned.

I thought about Carl Hilb and the big alligator, and I was silent.

Mrs. Blackert left me alone in that spooky room. I sat in the flickering candlelight while those eerie people in the windows—or were they ghouls?—jeered at me. I tried to tell myself that they weren't real. Surely no one could live within a pane of glass. Surely those images I saw were merely reflections of the candlelight. But each time I closed my eyes and reopened them, those leering people were there. I gazed at the floor. Shadows spun around my feet. I kept waiting for them to grasp my ankles, slither up my legs. I imagined that their grips would feel as cold as Mrs. Blackert's hands.

Maybe Cara will come back for me, I thought hopefully. Maybe she'll return with the police. But I wasn't even sure if Cara had made it home. Perhaps the cats had captured her.

I peered outside, forcing myself to look beyond the window ghouls. I saw the bleak, knotty outlines of the leafless trees and, beyond them, the moon. The moon looked very strange. It was still bright and white in most places, yet a deep orange shading had appeared on its lower right side.

"The answers are in the universe," Mrs. O had once told me.

But were they?

Hirst's Portrait

Mrs. Blackert reappeared carrying Doug Hirst III's portrait. She placed it on the easel.

She smiled diabolically at both of us, and then she threw back her arms, lifted her jaw into the air, and let out a long, indulgent yawn. For several seconds she blinked wearily. This surprised me. I thought she'd be energized, thrilled by the prospect of punishing me. Instead, I got the feeling that it was way past her bedtime.

"Since you were so helpful, my dear, I'll see to you first," she told Hirst between yawns.

Hirst grinned at her delightedly.

I expected Mrs. Blackert to get out that jar of crystalline liquid she'd used to free Cara, but she didn't do that. She took out a splotchy palette, a few tubes of paint, several white-bristled brushes, and some jars of liquid, all of which she arranged around the easel. I glanced at Hirst to see if he thought this was odd, but he was still grinning away like a hyena.

Mrs. Blackert opened a tube and began to paint, her brush swishing to the left of Hirst. Black paint appeared on the canvas. What on earth was Mrs. Blackert doing?

She painted very slowly. As she painted, she grew very drowsy. Her eyes drooped, then struggled to reopen, and frequently she stopped to yawn and rub her eyes.

I suppose Hirst was so close to her paintbrush that he couldn't really see what she was doing. Even if he could have, I don't think it would've mattered. Unlike me, Hirst didn't know *how* she freed people. There was no way for him to realize that she was not keeping her promise.

"Come on, old girl," he goaded Mrs. Blackert, "don't fall asleep on me. Not now, not when I'm almost free."

On and on, for perhaps an hour, Mrs. Blackert painted.

"How's it coming?" Hirst finally asked her. "How much longer till I'm out of this thing?"

Mrs. Blackert didn't respond. She merely dipped her brush into a dollop of paint and smiled mysteriously.

I could've answered his question. I could've told Hirst that the painting was coming along quite nicely. I could've told him that he would never be free. I saw quite clearly that Mrs. Blackert was painting a big black cat into his portrait. But I didn't say a word. I remained obediently silent.

By the time the panther was finished, Mrs. Blackert appeared so tired, I was certain she'd never have the energy to paint me. She put down her brush and took several steps backward to survey her work.

"You mean you're done?" Hirst shouted. "So when do I get out?"

A devilish grin spread across Mrs. Blackert's lips.

"Look," she told him. She pointed a paint-splattered finger at the crouched panther.

Hirst, realizing for the first time that he had been tricked, paled. Slowly, fearfully, he turned his crumbly yellow head.

"AHHHH!" he screeched when he saw the panther. "But you promis—"

He didn't get to finish, because the very moment he opened his mouth, the panther rose on its haunches. I was sure it was going to pounce, but Mrs. Blackert stopped it, saying, "Wait!"

The panther slinked back, its eyes never leaving Hirst.

"You must be dotty if you thought I would ever free a dirty rat like you," Mrs. Blackert told Hirst evenly. "It is a pity, really. All these years and you have not changed one bit. At least now I will not have to hear any of your blather. If you ever utter so much as a sound, you will be a scratching post for that great black cat."

Hirst's thin lips quivered and his eyes bulged out of their sockets, but he remained uncharacteristically silent.

My Portrait

Mrs. Blackert turned to me.

"As for you, my young friend, do not think I have forgotten you," she said. She folded her arms. "If only you

156

had respected my wishes, you would have had your Cara and your life. Instead you defied me, so . . ."

I gulped. I knew the rest.

"I am going to return my sweet husband to his place on the wall. But I assure you, my dear, I will be back."

For about the hundredth time she yawned. Then she picked up Doug Hirst's picture frame and disappeared.

I sat in that uncomfortable chair trying to think of ways to escape. I could wiggle the chair across the floor, but that would be noisy. Besides, what would I do when I reached the stairs? I could scream for help, but no one besides Mrs. Blackert would hear me.

Then I remembered a story Cara had once told me about a famous magician.

"He could get out of anything," she'd said. "Once they tied the guy up, locked him in a chest, and chucked the chest into the water. And guess what? He got out! You see, what he did was as soon as they tied him up, he tensed his muscles to stretch the ropes, and relaxed his muscles to slacken them. He did this over and over again until the ropes loosened. Then he slipped out of them, unlocked the chest, and was free! The whole secret," Cara had added, "is to stay calm."

She'd had me tie her to a chair so she could try this technique herself, but after ten minutes of tensing and relaxing, she got frustrated, wobbled the chair, and fell over.

"Get me out of here," she'd growled from the floor. I'd had to cut her loose with scissors.

Since I didn't have any other options, I tensed my arms and legs, counted to ten, then relaxed them. I repeated this about thirty times, till a little band of sweat appeared on my forehead. I thought I was making pretty decent progress when I heard footsteps on the stairs. Mrs. Blackert was returning. I was done for, history. Though the ropes around my wrists and ankles were looser, they weren't loose enough for me to escape.

I stared outside, toward freedom. Through a clump of skeletal trees I saw the faint glimmer of lights in my house. But my house looked as though it were miles away, in another world where witches didn't exist.

The moon appeared even more unusual than what I had seen earlier. Half of it shone like a bright white headlight. The other half was orange—a deep, rusty orange. Never before had I seen a moon like this.

"What are you looking at?" Mrs. Blackert snarled from the doorway, startling me. With her dreadful black eyes she followed my gaze. Suddenly her hands flew to her face. "It cannot be!" she cried.

I stared at her, dumbfounded. What had upset her so?

Her head whipped around. "There's still time," she muttered. She bounded into the room, pulled out a blank canvas, and plopped it down on the easel. She snatched at brushes and tubes and began to paint furiously.

I watched as her brush made a long flourish of yellow—my hair! I watched her mix reds, yellows, and whites to form my skin. Up, down, and around the paintbrush swished, forming my head and neck and the little curves of ears.

Mrs. Blackert seemed to be in a tremendous hurry to finish the painting. Quickly she formed the blue orbs of my eyes, the little hump of my nose, and the pink slash of my lips. Still, although she slapped paint onto the canvas like a madwoman, she seemed inexplicably tired, almost delirious. There were moments when her eyes closed completely, and her white head bobbed up and down like a buoy. Once she even dropped her paintbrush. Many times, more than I could count, she interrupted her painting to gaze anxiously outside. What disturbed her so?

I pondered this question, churned it over and over in my mind until, finally, I realized why the moon was slowly becoming orange—it was slipping into the Earth's shadow! We were in the midst of a lunar eclipse! Quite clearly I remembered Mr. Hadaway telling me earlier that a lunar eclipse would take place on this very night!

A shiver of sheer delight ran though me as I recalled

Cara's words of many weeks ago—both lunar and solar eclipses, she'd said, deprive witches of their powers! Now I understood why Mrs. Blackert was in such a hurry to finish my portrait!

But when during a lunar eclipse did a witch lose her powers? Mrs. Blackert was growing groggier and groggier, but she hadn't stopped painting.

I studied my portrait. Already the girl in the canvas looked like me. All that was needed were details: the dark sweep of my eyelashes, the shape of my brows, the tiny brown mole on the side of my chin. How much longer did I have until I became one with it? Perhaps when Mrs. Blackert finished my eyes. Or perhaps later, when she added my mole. Cara hadn't entered her portrait until it was complete. Maybe there was still time.

Mrs. Blackert was working on the contours of my face, shaping my brows, forming the smooth curves of my cheekbones—when all of a sudden she slumped to the floor. The entire moon had slipped behind a brilliant red-orange curtain.

I was so happy, I wanted to cry, and yet I was still bound to the chair.

Outside, the stars gleamed in the strangely lit sky. How long did a lunar eclipse last? How much time did I have to escape? I didn't know.

Before me, in a white-and-black heap, Mrs. Blackert snored loudly. I tried not to listen to her. I tried not to gaze at my almost completed portrait. I tried to think only of freeing myself, of tensing and releasing my muscles.

I flexed. I relaxed. Time passed. I could almost hear the minutes ticking away. My neck and back ached, my muscles burned. I was unbearably hot in my purple parka. But I was in good shape from tennis. Slowly, I made progress. Gradually, the ropes loosened. But they weren't loose enough to slip out of.

Almost, I told myself, but not quite.

Mrs. Blackert stirred on the floor. She opened and closed her mouth and let out a great big snort.

I gazed anxiously at the sky. A bright, white glow beamed in the lower right-hand portion of the moon. The moon was easing out of the Earth's shadow! The eclipse was ending! I was running out of time!

Panic surged within me. Mrs. Blackert stirred again. I twisted and wriggled, trying to fight my way out of the chair. The chair wobbled dangerously.

Stay calm, a voice in my head warned me. If I tipped the chair over, as Cara had done, I'd never get free.

I took a deep breath, then another and another. Gradually I calmed down. I tensed my muscles again. I relaxed them. Finally, miraculously, the ropes about my wrists loosened and slipped to the floor. My head throbbed and I was drenched with sweat, but I was almost free.

I extended my stiff and achy arms over my head, then bent down to untie my ankles. My fingers were scrambling over the ropes when Mrs. Blackert suddenly propped herself up. I looked at her, terrified. She gazed back at me, her eyes struggling to focus.

Quick, Laura, I told myself. My fingers tugged at the ropes frantically.

Mrs. Blackert rubbed her eyes and stretched her creaky limbs, while the orange curtain slipped away from the moon.

My ankles were free! I leaped to my feet.

At that very moment Mrs. Blackert rose. She slapped her face and stomped her feet in an effort to shake off her grogginess.

Run, I told myself. I ducked past Mrs. Blackert's wildly grasping hands and ran as fast as I could. Mrs. Blackert ran after me.

When I reached the bottom of the stairs, a bright-orange ball of fur flew at my face, shocking me. The cats—I had forgotten about them! Cats tore at my hair, clung to my parka, and wrapped themselves around my sore ankles, still I forged onward. I sprinted toward the front door, wrested it open, and staggered into the night. I guess Mrs. Blackert was quite close behind me, because when I slammed the door, I shut it on her hand. She let out a bloodcurdling cry. Hearing her, the stunned cats dropped to the ground. Mrs. Blackert's fingers twitched and twisted like octopus arms. "Come here," those fleshy white tentacles seemed to be saying. "Come back."

Though they were undeniably repulsive, there was something hypnotic about those squirming fingers. I knew if I stared at them for long, I'd never leave that stoop.

I turned and scurried down the slate path. Out of the corner of my eye I saw the dreadful ivy uncoil itself from the trees. It dropped to the ground and slithered after me. I heard it rustle through the leaves and hiss along the slate. I ran as I had never run before. I felt a tendril of ivy curl around my ankle. I leaped onto the sidewalk.

The Grabbing Hand

I was racing through the frosty night toward home when someone or something reached out and grabbed the back of my parka, causing me to stumble.

"Ahh!" I screamed as I crashed to the ground. Though my knees burned and my lungs ached, I crawled along the sidewalk in a desperate effort to escape.

"I'm almost there," I sobbed. "You can't get me now!"

I felt a great swat on my head.

"Shush, Laura!" It was Cara! It was she who had grabbed my parka. "You'll wake up the dead!"

163

She pulled me off the sidewalk and dragged me into the space between our brick wall and Mrs. Blackert's hedges. When we were several yards away from the sidewalk, she peered at me curiously through her old glasses.

"Gosh, you look awful, Laura. Like something the cat dragged in!"

"Very funny!" I panted, though I was certain she was right. Those cats had scratched me just about everywhere.

"You don't look so hot yourself," I told her. She didn't. She was still wearing that ridiculous witch costume and that black baseball hat. Her lips were blue.

"I've been waiting out here for hours," Cara whispered. "I almost froze to death. What took you so long, huh?"

My eyes searched the sidewalk and street for those awful cats and the slithering ivy. But to my relief both the sidewalk and street were clear.

"She got me," I told her.

"I figured that, Laura."

"Well if you knew that, then why didn't you come rescue me!" I practically shouted.

"Shush. I figured you'd get away. Because I saw the lunar eclipse."

"Yes. Well, I hate to tell you this, Cara, but that lunar eclipse took an awfully long while to affect Mrs. Blackert. If she hadn't taken time out to paint a panther into Doug Hirst's portrait, I'd be hanging on her wall right now!"

Cara frowned. "What's this about a panther?"

I explained.

"Wow!" She shook her head. "Well, he had it coming to him, you know." She chewed on her nail for a minute, then said, "I guess I owe you an apology, Laura. I goofed. According to that witch book I read, witches are supposed to be powerless throughout *all* the stages of an eclipse, not just during the main part. But I guess that's not true." She looked thoughtful for a moment, then added, "I ought to write the author a letter so he can get his facts straight."

"Why don't you do that," I muttered. I turned toward my house. I was cold and I was tired and I hurt. I wanted to go home.

Cara grabbed my arm. "Listen, Laura, we can't tell anyone about Mrs. Blackert!" I began to protest, but she silenced me.

"Look, Laura, if we tell our families about her, there's no telling what she'll do to them. She's one dangerous witch!"

"She *is* dangerous. That's exactly why we should tell," I argued.

But Cara disagreed. "Do you want to put your whole

family in danger? I don't! Gosh, my father and Nimbo are all I have! If something happened to them . . ." Her voice broke.

"Okay, okay," I told her. I didn't want her getting all sappy on me.

"Thanks, Laura," she said. "You're a real pal."

Together we hurried to my house.

When we reached my door, I turned to Cara and said, "What *are* you going to tell your dad and everyone else when they ask where you've been all this time?"

"I'll just say I can't remember, that's all. I'll say I just found myself wandering around on the street dressed in my Halloween costume."

"Speaking of streets," I said, staring down the dark, silent street toward her house, "do you want to call your dad to pick you up?"

"Nah, your mother will ask too many questions." She smiled briefly, then bolted for home.

The Lie

When I burst through the kitchen door, my father was on the phone with the police reporting me missing.

"She's a skinny kid with long blond . . . Laura!" he yelled when he saw me. The phone dropped out of his hand. It swung back and forth on its cord like a yo-yo. I leaned against the door and sighed.

My mother, Lucy, and even Mrs. O, who'd rushed over the minute she learned I was missing, were seated at the kitchen table.

Lucy spat out the hair she'd been munching on and exclaimed, "What happened to you?"

Oh how I wanted to tell them the truth! Mrs. Blackert was too big a problem for two twelve-year-old kids to handle. But when I saw their concerned faces, I remembered Cara asking me whether I wanted to put them all in danger.

So I took a deep breath and said, "I was on my way over to Mr. Hadaway's with the tacos when I heard a commotion in the graveyard. I went to investigate and wound up right smack in the middle of this nasty dog-and-cat fight. The dog charged at me. I guess I passed out, because when I woke up, I was sprawled across a grave and the taco bag was gone!"

Everyone stared at me for a moment. Then my mother wailed, "And you wonder why I don't like animals!" For once she didn't ask a million questions. Instead, she got up and started checking me for bites.

My father picked up the phone and said, "I ought to report those stray beasts to the police. They *were* strays—you didn't recognize them from the neighborhood, did you, Laura?"

"No," I said quietly.

Mrs. O studied me with narrowed eyes and puckered lips. She sniffed the air, as if she smelled something fishy.

"Sounds like another one of your stories, Laura," Lucy muttered skeptically.

Cara's Question

Thursday at school I told everyone the same story about the cat and the dog and the graveyard. For a day I was sort of a celebrity. Though I had tennis practice that afternoon, I took the early bus home. I was too achy to swing a racket. Being brave had definitely taken its toll on me.

When I got home, I crawled into bed and tried to do my homework, but I was so tired, I wound up taking a nap. I slept right through dinner, till the next morning!

Despite all that sleep, I was still worn out on Friday. Eliza and Jan asked me to go roller-skating with them after school, but I just didn't have the energy. I went right home and crept into bed with Bongo Bear. I read books and watched movies and tried very hard to forget about Mrs. Blackert. The problem was, I couldn't forget. Her unruly white hair and glittering black eyes were imprinted in my brain. Each time the doorbell chimed, I was certain she had come for me. Each time the phone rang, I picked it up expecting to hear her voice hissing on the other end of the line. I couldn't forget Mrs. Blackert because I knew she hadn't forgotten me.

Shortly before dinner the doorbell rang. I flew out of bed and rushed to my bedroom door. I opened it a crack. And I breathed an enormous sigh of relief.

"Why, Cara," I heard Mrs. O declare. Poor Cara, Mrs. O didn't sound at all happy to see her.

I hopped back into bed and listened as footsteps approached my bedroom door.

Mrs. O knocked. "Laura," she called, "Cara is here! Do you wish to see her?"

"Sure," I replied, my heart quickening.

A second later Cara stepped into my room wearing baggy jeans and an oversized sweatshirt. She carried a big, shapeless jacket in one of her arms. "Hi!" she said cheerfully.

I leaned over and turned my radio on loud so Mrs. O couldn't overhear our conversation.

Cara tossed her jacket on the floor and plopped down at the edge of my bed. She glanced at the books on my nightstand then pushed up her glasses. They were her old glasses, the intellectual ones with the thin gold frames.

I pointed to my closet. "Your new glasses are in there. In the Scrabble box. I'm sorry, but I ate all your Halloween candy."

"It probably would've been stale by now anyhow."

169

She strolled over to my closet, opened the door, and rummaged around until she found her new glasses. She put them on and stared at herself in my mirror.

"Cool," she said to her reflection.

She slipped her old glasses into a pocket of her jeans, then sat back down on my bed. She did look better in her new cat glasses, less nerdy, more with-it.

Cara sighed. "Listen, Laura, I want to thank you for getting me out of that spook joint. If you hadn't rescued me, I would've gone bonkers. I think my father and Nimbo would've gone crazy too." She told me how her father just about jumped out of his skin when he saw her standing outside the cottage door.

"You should've seen his smile," she said. "It was so big and wide and wiggly, I thought it'd fall right off his face. Nimbo was pretty ecstatic too. He flew out of that dirt hole and started dancing around in circles. I think he would've wasted away if you hadn't saved me from that witch." Cara picked up one of the books on my nightstand and examined it. It was a book about a boy and his two dogs. "No more vampire books, huh?" she asked with a smile.

"I've had enough horror for now," I told her.

She flipped through the pages, but I could tell she wasn't really reading them. She was just looking for something to do with her hands. She had something on her mind.

170

Finally she put the book down and said, "Speaking of horror . . ."

I sank deeper into my pillows and groaned.

"I was just wondering if you could tell me how Mrs. Blackert got me out of that portrait. That's all."

I sat up and stared at her hard. "You mean you didn't see what she was doing?"

"Uh-uh. I couldn't. I could tell she was doing something with her hair, but she was so close to me that everything seemed distorted."

Something—call it intuition—warned me that I shouldn't tell Cara how Mrs. Blackert had freed her, that she was better off not knowing. But old persuasive Cara eventually forced the story out of me.

She listened, enrapt, while I described that strange room full of shadows and specters. I told her also about the rows of paintbrushes, the tendril of hair, and the jar of crystalline liquid.

"Wow!" she roared when I was finished.

"I have one final question for you," I said. "Did your father buy that crazy story you told him about how you just found yourself on the street?"

"I'm sure he thought it was weird," Cara replied. "But yeah, he bought it. He asked me if I wanted to see a shrink so I could, you know, get hypnotized. He thought maybe that would help jog my memory. I told him I just wanted to get on with my life."

171

Cara's News

At first Cara had a tough time getting on with her life. Television, newspaper, and magazine reporters swarmed around her like a pack of horseflies. They begged her to describe her ordeal. What eventually made them lose interest was the fact that there apparently was no ordeal, none that she said she could remember anyway.

As for me, I lived in a constant state of terror. Thanksgiving came and went; still I expected to see Mrs. Blackert's black-clad figure hovering on our front-door stoop. Still I dreaded the ring of the phone. And oh, how I loathed passing her big, gloomy house! I expected her to leap out of those monster hedges, her lips twisted into an evil grin, her hands grabbing at me.

Then, one Saturday in December, Cara, who hadn't mentioned Mrs. Blackert in a long time, gave me some surprising news. We were Christmas shopping, wandering in and out of festive town stores, when she said, "She went to England for the holidays. The postman told me."

"Who went to England?" I asked absently. I hadn't really been paying attention to her. I'd been eyeing a new tennis racket, debating whether I ought to put it on my list.

"Who do you think, Laura?"

All of a sudden I forgot about the racket, the store, and Christmas. "You mean . . ."

"I mean Mrs. Blackert, you numbskull."

"Well," I said quite haughtily, "if you think I'm going to—" I was going to say, "take one step inside that monstrous house," but Cara cut me off.

"I'm not asking you to go inside that house, Laura," she said. "I promised I'd never bug you about Mrs. Blackert again, and I meant it."

She was right; she did keep her promises.

"I'm simply telling you that she's gone so you won't get so freaky every time you pass her house."

"I don't . . . act . . . freaky," I protested.

Cara, who knew better, merely smirked at me.

Strange Occurrences

On Monday there was a terrible snowstorm. You could hardly see a thing outside—the windows looked as though they'd been swathed with white sheets. School was closed, so I stayed in all day devouring books.

Near dinnertime my family and I gathered around the tube to watch the latest news on the storm. The broadcast opened with the record snowfall and how much trouble it'd caused. Another story followed—a story that sent my head reeling.

In the middle of the blinding white afternoon, a family named Login had heard a knock on their door.

"Whoever it was," Mrs. Login told a redheaded television reporter, "just kept hammering away. I couldn't imagine who it could be. I mean, no one in their right mind would be out in this nasty weather!"

"Finally I opened the door," announced a burly, dark-haired man, who I guessed was Mr. Login, "and there was our long-lost daughter, Beth!"

I sat up in my seat, my eyes riveted to the TV. The camera flashed to Beth.

"Snake Eyes!" I cried.

"What'd you say?" Lucy turned to me and frowned.

"That's the girl who set my school on fire, the girl who disappeared!" I almost shouted. I was pretty worked up.

"Well, Laura, you don't have to throw a fit about it!" Lucy snapped.

The reporter went on to say what a strange coincidence it was that two girls from Dove's Cove had disappeared, only to be found in perfectly fine condition. "Where were you all this time?" she inquired, thrusting the microphone under Snake Eyes's little snub nose.

If Cara was watching this broadcast, she was surely snickering. She'd been asked the same question about a million times. She complained she even heard it in her sleep.

To my amazement, Snake Eyes told the reporter, "I was hanging on a wall in some witch's dining room."

"Excuse me?" the reporter stuttered. You could tell

this wasn't exactly what she'd expected old Snake Eyes to say.

"You heard me," said Snake Eyes, as hateful as ever.

The reporter was stumped. I mean, what *could* you say to a comment like that? Nothing. So she ended the interview. She said, "Well, that's all from here! Now back to the news desk for more on the storm!"

I sat in stunned silence, my brain struggling to make sense out of this new disclosure. How could Mrs. Blackert have freed Snake Eyes when she was in England? Clearly, given what I'd witnessed in that workroom of hers, she couldn't have accomplished this from across the sea. That meant only one thing—Mrs. Blackert was back!

I scurried to the phone.

"Cara," I panted when she answered, "did you see that report about Snake Eyes?"

"Yeah." She sounded bored.

"It means that Mrs. Blackert is back from England!" I blurted.

"Calm down, Laura. She's not back. She's a whole ocean away."

"But how can you be . . . she can't be . . . " I stammered.

"Just trust me, okay? She's in England. Look, I gotta go. We're watching a movie." She hung up. I was dumbstruck. She'd sounded so calm, so nonchalant, so certain that Mrs. Blackert was far, far away.

But if that was true, then who had set Snake Eyes free? And which of the other portraits had they unleashed?

I didn't have long to wait for an answer.

A Shocking Revelation

A couple of days later Cara and I were walking home from a movie when we noticed a bunch of vans and cop cars parked in front of Mrs. Blackert's house. A cluster of people stood around.

"What's going on?" I asked.

"There's only one way to find out," Cara replied, pulling me through the slushy snow.

A TV reporter was interviewing a policeman on the sidewalk.

When she saw the reporter, Cara yanked up her hood. She'd been doing that a lot lately. Whenever anyone looked like they recognized her from TV or the newspaper, she either hid in her clothes or slinked away. It was funny—she'd always wanted to be famous, and now that she was, she claimed that she wanted to be left alone.

The cop—a young, ruddy fellow—stared brazenly at the microphone. "Well," he said, "we were investigating that little girl's complaint. You know, Beth Login, the one who turned up out of nowhere. She insists that she was imprisoned by some lady named Black Heart."

I shot Cara a look.

The policeman went on, "Her tale was unusual, for sure. But we figured we better check it out anyway. Like I always say, you never know when you might be onto something.

"We narrowed Black Heart down to Blackert. That's who lives here, some old lady named Blackert.

"Only when we knocked on the door, no one answered. So we checked up on her, found out she's in England."

So Cara was right! Mrs. Blackert *was* in England! I glanced at her, but she wasn't paying any attention to me. She was staring at the cop and the reporter.

The cop shrugged his shoulders and said, "That old lady might be roaming the continents, but an investigation is an investigation. And this kid was adamant about where she'd been. So finally we broke into the house. Busted down the door." He smiled proudly.

"But we didn't find anything suspicious. Just a lot of antique furniture and paints. What was strange . . . well . . . the dining room had all these picture frames hanging on the walls. But the paintings themselves were blank, white canvases. Except for one. There was one portrait that was so ugly, I don't know why anyone would want to hang it."

"What sort of portrait?" asked the reporter.

"A picture of an old guy. Maybe he's a relative or something. And there's a big black panther kind of crouched in the distance. Looks like at any minute it might pounce on the old guy. Spooky!"

I gripped Cara's arm. We walked quickly past all the commotion.

We were almost at my house when I erupted. "She let them go! But why? And when?"

Cara said evenly, "She didn't let them go, Laura."

"How can you say that? What do you . . ." Then I got it. I gagged. Mrs. Blackert hadn't let those portraits go. Cara had!

"How could you?" I whispered.

"How could I not? How could I just leave those poor people in there? I had to do it, Laura. I freed them all except for Doug Hirst the Third. You were right, he really is evil. You should've seen his face when I was letting the other portraits go. He was crazed, Laura—he turned redder than Mrs. Blackert's drapes. Fortunately, because of that panther, he couldn't open his big mouth."

"But how did you do it?" I practically sobbed. "To free you, she used *her hair!*"

"Well, I used *my head*. You told me about those white-bristled paintbrushes in her workroom. I figured that the bristles had to have been made from Mrs.

Blackert's hair, and if that was true, they had to have the same magical powers. It was a long shot, I admit it, but I was right!"

I stared down at the watery slush and slowly shook my aching head. Of course Cara had been very clever. Who else would've figured out that those paintbrushes had been made from Mrs. Blackert's hair? Who else would've realized they had the same magical powers?

And, yet, at the same time, Cara had been foolish. She had failed to consider the consequences of her actions.

Mrs. Blackert would be furious when she discovered that her portraits were gone. She would blame Cara and me.

"We're doomed, Cara. Finished. Kaput," I muttered.

"Nonsense," she shot back. "That old hag can't do a thing to us, Laura. She doesn't have anything of ours— none of our personal possessions. Without them she can't stick us in portraits. We're home free."

New Year's Eve

Christmas came and went. Because my parents have this thing about tradition, we were spending New Year's Eve with the Benzers, at their house. Lucy and I were forced to attend. Heaven forbid we should do something else—like ring in the new year with our friends. No, each and every year we got all decked out in our good clothes, ate till our stomachs bulged, and then, at midnight, witnessed a bunch of silly adults running around with funny hats and horns and party streamers. What made it even worse was listening to Mary Jane describe, in detail, the New Year's Eve celebrations of all her favorite soap-opera characters. The very thought of New Year's Eve was enough to make me sick.

But being that I was nothing but a powerless kid, I didn't have much choice in the matter. So on this particular New Year's Eve I threw on a light-pink sweater, which my parents had given me for Christmas, and a short cream skirt. When Lucy, the clothes maven, saw my outfit, she made this horrendous squealing noise and cried, "Oh, I have the perfect lipstick for you, Laura!" Before I knew it, she was smearing "candy pink" lipstick across my lips.

"You look amazing," she said, studying me, the tube still poised dangerously in her hand. "I hope there are some cute little boys at the party." I grunted. *Little boys!* Give me a break—I was twelve!

When my mother saw me in my pink sweater and matching lipstick, she just about flipped out. "Our little girl is growing up," she gushed to my father. "Laura, you simply must wear your new cream coat and . . . and those fuzzy pink gloves I got you last year! They match your sweater. Oh, how adorable you'll look."

"Yeah, yeah, yeah," I grumbled.

My parents and Lucy were all set to go. They were waiting for me. I plodded over to the front-hall closet and slipped on the cream coat, another Christmas gift from my parents. My mother said it was made out of the wool of an alpaca, which made it extra light and soft and warm. But those pink gloves—where were they? I searched our glove-and-scarf bin. No luck.

"Hurry, Laura!" called my mother.

"I can't find my gloves!" I shouted. The night was off to a rotten start.

"Well, where did you put them?" my mother hollered back.

"Now if I knew that," I mumbled, "I wouldn't be having this problem!" Then it hit me. It hit me hard, like an icy snowball. I'd stuffed my fuzzy pink gloves into the pockets of my parka the night I'd visited Mrs. Blackert.

I ran to the closet, pushed through the row of coats, and found the puffy purple fabric. I grabbed one of the ravaged arms. Feathers flew out of the slits and tickled my nose. I stuck my hand inside one of the flannel pockets. I found an old, lint-covered Tootsie Roll, a dime, and a hair band, but no gloves.

My head began to pound. My mother called to me again, but there was so much throbbing in my ears, I couldn't hear what she was saying.

I reached into the other pocket. My fingers touched

something fuzzy. I pulled it out. It was a glove. One fuzzy pink glove. I stuck my hand back into the pocket and groped around, but aside from an old crumpled gum wrapper, the pocket was empty. I yanked the parka out of the closet and searched to see if there was a hole in the pocket—perhaps the glove had fallen into the lining of the coat. But there was none.

A numbing horror overtook me as I explored the closet floor and hunted through boots, sneakers, and shoe polish. I didn't find my missing glove.

I floated back into the kitchen, the one glove I had found dangling from my fingers. My family was already outside, waiting for me in the car. Listlessly, like a sleepwalker, I locked the side door and staggered into the harsh grip of winter.

My father had backed the car to the end of our driveway. It sat there, huffing gray exhaust into the dead, frosty air. It was as I tottered down the driveway toward our car that I saw the limousine. It slithered around the corner like a long black snake, settling just outside Mrs. Blackert's house. I froze.

A man dressed from head to toe in black got out of the driver's seat. He walked around the long, sleek, serpentine car and opened one of the doors. Out poured cats. Orange cats. Thirteen of them. Like a rusty stream, they spilled onto the snowy curb. They shook themselves, and—I'm sure of it—each and every one of them cast a sly glance my way.

Next Mrs. Blackert, adorned in her flowing black cape and a wide black hat, emerged. For a moment she stood in the snow and regarded her vacant house. Then she moved her hand—the one closest to me—to the pocket of her cape. She tilted her head my way and smiled as only a witch can smile.

And as she moved toward her house with a ghostly fluidity, I was certain that I saw, between her black gloved fingers, something peeking out. Something fuzzy and pink.

And so began my new year.